TOYOKO

ED GILBERT

Order this book online at www.trafford.com
or email orders@trafford.com

Most Trafford titles are also available at major online book retailers.

Printed in the United States of America.

ISBN: 978-1-4907-5181-8 (sc)
ISBN: 978-1-4907-5183-2 (hc)
ISBN: 978-1-4907-5182-5 (e)

Library of Congress Control Number: 2014921271

Trafford rev. 11/25/2014

www.trafford.com
North America & international
toll-free: 1 888 232 4444 (USA & Canada)
fax: 812 355 4082

ACKNOWLEDGEMENTS

A special "thank you" must go to my friend, Gerry Vandlen, without whose assistance during its preparation this book could not be published.

It seems also appropriate to thank the United States Marine Corps. By their orders, I was to experience a 13-month tour of duty in the country of Japan.

Too numerous to name are the many Japanese people met during this adventure. Actually, they caused me to understand that they are really not so different from families and individuals in the United States.

Ed Gilbert

CHAPTER ONE

Lieutenant Miller poked his red-lidded head through the open hatch leading to our squadbay and someone standing nearby yelled "Tenn-Shunn!" I scrambled from my sack as the bay suddenly turned quiet.

"At ease, men." Miller glanced to either side, then grinned before continuing, "Well, you probably all know what the score is by now. We'll more than likely be here in Kobe for a few weeks while the Navy repairs this tub. No straight dope on it as of now, but scuttlebutt has it that we'll be billeted somewhere off the ship…Hell! I hope so!"

He appeared pleased at the chuckles this received, then continued, "I do know for sure that we're to be harnessed up and have the platoon formed on deck in half an hour." He glanced at his watch and then up at me. "Sergeant Gillaney, better put a few men to work cleaning up the area. If we leave the ship looking like it does now, the Navy'll have me by the tail, an' you guys by something else! That's all! Be on deck and in platoon formation by fourteen-hundred."

When Miller had gone I detailed three men for a sweep-down and began repacking my molding sea bag. As I tossed the stuff into the bag, I thought over this misfortune with a growing distaste…Talk about a ripple on the lagoon of happiness! Three weeks aboard a stinking ship loaded with 2,000 Marines, bad weather, ill tempers, and now this! Tying into a Japanese harbor didn't seem very impressive.

We had been on the General Perry for more than a week over the normal run from 'Frisco' to Korea. Our converted old tanker had lost one of its screws beyond the point of no return so we had been creeping along at a slow ten-knot clip. I tried to draw some consolation from the thought that this lay-over would undoubtedly be cooler than the welcome waiting the remainder of our convoy at its destination…But I had wanted to go to Korea. Hell! I should have joined the Army!

I was still cursing things in general when a high-pitched voice filtered through from several aisles away. It was Private Harris addressing someone. "Listen man, this is the best damn thing that's happened to me since I got my stripes back! I was stationed in Japan back in '47, and I'll bet things haven't changed a damned bit…First thing I'm going to do when I fly this trap is head for Tokyo – I got a gal there that's been cry'n her eyes out for me for years"

I had little or no compassion for the squirt to begin with, and his remark only served up additional dis-flavor. I'd heard a few stories about Japanese women, and rather abruptly, but not I figured prematurely, concluded that half of my men would desert before we would ship out for Korea again. At least I could certainly count on Harris and a few of his ear-bent buddies.

"Harris, if you don't shut up and get busy packing, I'll personally see that you don't leave the ship…The captain needs a few men aboard for mess duty!" I turned from my general direction and took some of my wrath out on the sagging sea bag, degrading each and every item and moment between then and when we had the platoon formed on the deck of the transport.

We were quickly herded into a row of Quonset huts that were situated several hundred yards from the dock, the type with the cold and damp cement floors that World War II had popularized. But the Navy did its worst to make us comfortable. Showers had previously been installed and a temporary PX was quickly set up in one of the huts, where beer was the prime attraction.

Thus far no one could tell, at least from our vantage point, that we had arrived on foreign soil, and a cry for liberty went up. No reply was heard from the C.O.'s office, which immediately brought forth a multitude of useless protests and additional suffixes to the Company Commander's name. I concluded that I didn't give a damn one way or the other as far as liberty in this port was concerned. Retrieving a second-rate Western that someone had appropriately discarded on the lid of a trash can, I settled down on my bunk to wait it out.

About 16:00 the following afternoon an orderly walked into the hut and approached me. "Captain Bartlett wants you over in his office right away." I thanked him rather hesitantly as he left, jumped off the bunk and looked down at my wrinkled fatigues. To heck with the clothes, it was an immediate order. Maybe things aren't going to take so long after all. I could be going on ahead to Korea with a special group, or perhaps we'd all be going right away. The fact that I'd have probably been the last person he'd call to share that formidable information with didn't occur to me and I sharpened my step as I entered the Company Commander's office.

Captain Bartlett sat half-hunched over in the bamboo chair behind the bamboo desk, chewing on what remained of a Havana. No one had ever recalled seeing him without the stogie, with the exception of formations, and he never lit it but instead bobbed it about his face as he chewed it down to a stump. He always wore a uniform so neat that it made him appear ready to pose for a magazine cover, and he didn't appear any different this time.

His greying head snapped up and he gave me no time for a salute. "No formalities, Sergeant. Take a seat over there." He waved me to another cane-bottomed chair beside the desk and I sat down on the edge of it. He deliberately thumbed through a stack of papers for a moment and then turned to me. "Sergeant, you're not here for a chewing-out, or here for a medal if that will help put you at ease." He saw me stiffen in the chair, and continued, "I have your service records here and I've gone over them. Let's lay it right on the line for you. Marine Division Headquarters is right here in Japan, at Camp Garu. They told us this morning that they've a problem: Their G-3 section is in need of a man for their Topographic Department. Their man just headed for the States on emergency leave, and his time was about up over here anyway, so he's not coming back. By any means, they need a replacement immediately." He paused, letting his words sink in. I waited for what I knew was coming, and it did. "We have two of you in the Battalion, but the 'specs' call for a Sergeant. That means you're it."

My blood pressure and bad attitude had risen considerably, and sensing this, he hastened, "I know you don't like the idea of all this but we have no choice in the matter. Your orders are being cut right now – pick them up at the Battalion H.Q. They'll iron out any other details while you're over there…you have three days' time before you're to report at Camp Garu." He ended abruptly, still looking directly at me, only now his expression took on one of defense, as though he were looking at a smoking volcano that he expected to erupt any minute.

3

It was a futile situation and I knew it. I was furious and my very nature told me to jump up and protest – 'Let's face it,' my mind was saying, 'this is City Hall for you and you've had it.' I drew my slouching 5'10" frame up from the chair in a listless movement and asked simply, "Will that be all, sir?"

His face took on an expression of amazement for a moment and then changed to a smile as he arose and moved around the edge of the desk. "Yes, that's all," then as almost an after-thought, "And Gillaney, before you storm out of here thinking of me as a prime target that you'd like to shoot to bits on the range, I'll tell you that I've discussed this with Lieutenant Miller and been made aware of your desire to go to Korea. Well, rumor has it, mind you, it's only rumor, that the Third Division is about to be sent over too, probably within three or four months." He extended his hand and I shook it rather listlessly as he ended it with "Good luck, and I expect to see you again someday."

I left the shack. It had all been so simple for Captain Bartlett…"We haven't any choice in the matter." Hey, what about some choice for me! I hadn't even put a word in edgewise. The fact that it was part of the Captain's job and that he probably hadn't enjoyed it didn't occur to me, as mentally I kicked both of us all the way to the Battalion Headquarters.

* * * *

The train was cramped and much smaller than any I'd been on in the States, but it was moving along at a terrific pace. I felt conspicuous and nervous and could imagine how I must appear to the Japanese people….. my medium height and 170 pounds of Marine, sitting uneasily, in olive drab uniform, blue eyes that were quite uncommon to this country's local populace, a red-freckled face bedecked by brown hair that I knew was protruding awkwardly in several directions from under a slightly-cocked service cap. Then I lost some of my self-consciousness and upon peering around, discovered that not one of the several people aboard even seemed to have noticed me.

Directly opposite sat an old woman. Her grey hair and wrinkled face bobbed up and down and sideways as the train moved. She wore a red kimono that came down to her ankles, where it met a pair of black wooden shoes that were openly suspended from her big toe and also bobbed to and fro with the music of the train wheels. She was sound asleep. Two men sat nearby. They were engrossed in a low conversation and never looked my way. One of them was dressed in a black suit and wore a hat; the other was dressed in clothes that would remind one of a farmer. The latter kept nodding and uttering "Hi" as he flashed a row of gold teeth toward the leader of their conversation.

So what? So what if all this was strange? What of it if the other occupants were of quaint dress and tongue? I wasn't ready to accept any part of the idea anyway....it would take the better part of four hours to arrive at Camp Garu, so I settled down dispiritedly as though trying to prolong the realization that I was in a strange land by casting it from my view.

* * * *

It was night, and it was warm. I felt myself slowly succumbing to the gentle clickity-clack of the wheels. They reminded me somewhat of the times I had sat and sleepily fished off the railroad bridge over the South Branch River....that has been a long time ago. Then the clicking gave way slowly to a distant hum that gradually became the deafening roar of a crowd. The football stadium in the center of the State Campus came into focus. It was September, the early winter wind was crisp, and the red and brown leaves were beginning to fall earthward in gentle spirals.

CHAPTER TWO

I'd showered and returned to the dormitory after the game. I had a raincoat draped around me for some protection and Bill looked up with his usual silly grin as I entered our room. "Well, do enter, ladies! Oh, I declare! It isn't a chick under that hood at all; it's our national hero!"

"And just what's all that garble supposed to mean, Doc?" I turned and hung the coat on a hook by the closet, knowing full-well what was coming next.

"Oh, just a meaningless little pun, that's all. Besides, don't play coy with me, buddy – it'll be a 'cold' day when you score a couple of T.D.'s and pass for another in one afternoon and can't take a little rib." He flung the magazine he had been reading and it fluttered off my shoulder as I ducked. "Look at your head, Hero ... it even looks like a football, what with being pointed on both ends and all!"

I couldn't help but grin. "OK, so I'm proud. I just hope the Press gives me a better build-up than you just did! One helluva PR man you'd make! I won't deny that the 'pro' teams like All-Americans, and that's what I want...But right now I'm dead tired, so lay off the wise cracks."

I started to sit down on the bed. He thumped his fingers on the desk rather methodically for a moment; then, not looking up, "So while you're relaxing on your laurels, who's gonna do that experiment for you over at the Lab? Einstein, perhaps?"

"Good Grief!" I stood up and looked at him, hopelessly. "Professor Werner'll have my tail if that thing isn't finished by Monday. I should have stayed in the lab and finished it last night. Just too damn beat." I started to get up. "Well, another glorious Sunday shot to hell!"

He looked my way this time with a serious expression. "Never mind Hero, it's done. Been over there all afternoon. I had to do the same one you've been working on…I heard the game on the radio, and, by the way, that last seventy-two yarder you ran nearly made me flop the whole damn experiment. Give more warning next time, will you? Whistle or something so I don't start jumping up and down with a breaker of HCLO-3 in my hands!"

I nearly grabbed the little brain and hugged him. "Listen, Doc, someday, after you and I are both famous, I'm gonna point your way and say, 'There goes that brilliant Doctor Lugan, without whose help I never could've risen to the great height of prosperity – as a garbage collector!'"

"That's OK, Trash, I'll simply tell the truth," he smirked. "While that joker was playing around with a football, I was doing his chemistry experiments. And believe it or not, Ripley, that's how I learned something and became an M.D.!"

I said seriously, "You know something, Bill? I bet you'll make it too." I took off everything but my shorts and t-shirt and stretched out on my sack. "On the level, Bill, Thanks."

He looked at me out of the corner of his eyes, "Don't crap out completely; I haven't given you the real message yet.

I straightened. "What message?"

"Babs, I mean Barbara, she only called twice in the past twenty minutes. That gal apparently just can't understand that a man doesn't run around all afternoon on a football field without taking time to shower some of the sweat off afterward. Sure wish I had a redhead like that nuts over me. Anyway, I told her you'd call back."

"Well, what the heck did you tell her that for? I'm pooped! Whose side are you on anyway?"

"Who's side? Ha! You're a joke! But in case you've had a sudden lapse of memory, it's Saturday afternoon and you two have a heavy dancing date tonight. She's just looking after her property, that's all. Of course, if you'd rather sit this one out on the bench, I might consider subbing for a few plays. Who knows, I might even score!"

I flung the magazine back at his grinning kisser, reached for the phone and then said, "You're o.k., Bill, but there's just one thing that bothers me."

"Huh? What's that?"

"What the hell is HCLO-3?

* * * *

It was dark and the old '39 Mercury's lamps weren't helping much as we bounced to the top of Desperation Point. Several cars were scattered about, so I picked a spot under a tree and killed both lights and engine.

We often drove up to 'The Point' after going out. We could be alone, do a little serious necking, or just plain talk.

Somehow it had never gone much farther than that….We'd known each other only two months, but already there was a spark between us. I jokingly told her that it felt like A-C meeting D-C, but I really had difficulty grasping just what the spark was.

Barbara was a pretty girl, but there was more. She had a personality about her that made things happen to me, and the feeling had never stopped, not since that very first dance together back in October.

This evening she wasn't her usual talkative self, but instead quietly clung to me, seldom talking, her head on my shoulder. We had stayed at the dance until eleven and I was wondering why I went in the first place. Barbara was a trifle on the snobbish side though, and I guessed that she was showing me off a little. It seemed that she was always dragging me off to places I never really wanted to go, but then I never turned her down.

"What's bothering you, Babs?" I turned in the seat and hung my arm over her shoulder.

It was some time before she answered. Finally she lifted her eyes up to mine. "Have you ever loved anyone before, Gil? I mean, really loved them?" The hesitating question, coupled with the look behind it, made me wither a little. Her eyes were trying to read mine and I took a deep breath before answering. Realizing that she was leading into something we had both managed to avoid up to now made it even worse.

"There were the usual girls, but I doubt if I ever classified it as love." I felt nervous and rather awkward and I knew that she was going to say what I feared, yet really wanted to hear.

She was toying with a button on my shirt as she looked up again. "It isn't easy to explain, Gil. It's something I've never known before…like a hard lump deep inside, a feeling I've been afraid of ever since I met you." She was speaking my thoughts as well as her own. I could never bring myself to tell her….And now she had told me. I had shoved those same emotions from my mind so many times. I hadn't mentioned anything about love to her. I hadn't even admitted it to myself.

"What I'm trying to say is that I love you...I may be making a fool out of myself but I love you more than anything else in the world, Gil. Do you love me?" Tears slowly formed as her eyes questioned me. I peered at her and suddenly knew that I did love her, loved her and wanted her more than anything I had ever dreamed of. I searched frantically for words, words that could explain the sudden urge within me, but there were none to be found.

"Yes, Barbara, I love you," I finally stammered.

We embraced and kissed as we never had before. I was burning with a feverish passion that rendered me unconscious of anything but her closeness and femininity, and our desire for one another became overpowering. Her whole body was twisting and thrusting against mine as though it were freeing itself of an internal agony. Her moist lips parted as she ran the tip of her tongue around the lobe of my ear.

"Oh Gil, I love you! I love you so! I want you now!" There was an urgent and uncontrollable desire in each of us for unrestrained love, as we pressed outward in the seat of the car to free ourselves of the enclosing elements that seemed to be fighting and hindering our movements.

CHAPTER THREE

Those next few months were a constant whirlwind of love. We probably should have been married then, but we put it off, rationalizing that marriage at that point would put a damper on our educations.

Time passed swiftly and June was nearing, along with the end of the term. She had casually promoted the idea that we could be married in the summer and in the Fall I could continue with my schooling while she found a job, an idea that I was agreeing with more and more.

However, the papers were jammed full of articles on the Korean War, now waging in full scale. I had been casually considering joining the service. Many of the boys were leaving after the school year, and the more I talked and came in contact with them, the more the idea grew. When I finally got up the courage to break it to Barbara, we were sitting on a bench in front of the chapel. She reacted angrily.

"Gil! No! What in the world are you thinking of? What of college? And us? You must be kidding!" It was as demanding a rebuttal as her personality and I tried to explain my feelings.

"No Barb, I'm not kidding at all. Of course I haven't done anything rash yet, but I've considered joining. As for you and me, that wouldn't change anything. We can still be married, and I can pick up my education later on. Besides, I'd feel like a draft dodger, going to school and dodging football players while a lot of my friends are over there dodging bullets. That hardly seems fair to me."

She looked at me tearfully then and said, "Gil, I want you for a husband. I don't care if you are a draft dodger, or a coward or whatever you might think. I just want you alive!"

I pulled her to her feet and kissed her gently. "We'll just forget the whole thing for the time being. There's plenty of time anyway."

I did forget the idea for the moment, but a week later it came back with startling swiftness. The hometown weekly paper arrived and I picked it up casually and began reading.

There was a column near the center of the page, along with a picture. The caption read, "Silver Star Awarded Local Mother Thursday." Under the photo it read, "Mrs. Florence Renay has received word from the Adjutant General that her son Arnold has been awarded posthumously, by direction of the President, the Silver Star for gallantry in action on June 1st, near Chung Bolguk, Korea…"

There was more but I could read no further as the mist covered my eyes. Oh, no! Not Arnold! Anybody but him! Only yesterday I had received another letter from my old buddy. I fumbled for it in the desk drawer and when I had located it, I sat there unbelieving and blinked at it again. The words became more blurred as I went along.

> Somewhere in Korea
> Date Unknown

Dear Gil,

By now I suppose you're pretty busy with exams. I sure wish I was there taking them, too. I don't regret joining the service, but I certainly wasn't expecting a war like this one.

We have lost eight men from our Company, and a lot of them have only about forty or fifty left. Seems like they have us outnumbered about ten to one, but every other man here has an automatic weapon. Sometimes they come over the hills so thick that you can't even see the ground, and I've seen them piled three deep in places and still coming!

I wish things would slack off so I could come back home, but I'm not really planning on it. If you see any of the other guys, like Jack or Whitey, or anyone, even girls, have them drop me a few lines when they get time. I'm not saying that I'll be able to answer them right away, but I will just as soon as I get time.

Well, I don't have much time and I have to leave, so will close.

> Your buddy,
> Arnold

I was trembling as I thought. My God! Here I've been sitting on my can like a patsy while all this has been going on! What am I, anyway! I pondered that question only a moment, then threw on my jacket and headed downtown for the recruiting office.

Barbara took the news as though she had been hit with a ton of bricks, and I explained to her as best I could with very little tact. She never really came around to my way of thinking. I was certain of that but could only hope that she would, in time, understand.

I went to boot camp in San Diego immediately after the close of the term, and we kept in a fair state of contact by mail. It was strange how a letter could be so vague and distant. It never seemed as though it was really Barbara talking when I read them. I could always imagine how much different it would be if she were saying the words in person.

After three months of intense training, I was given a fifteen-day leave. I was picking up my orders and airplane tickets home when I decided to buy her the ring. It was a beautiful solitaire, and upon getting home I immediately presented it to her. After that night we were again caught up in a whirlwind of love. In fact, those last two weeks together were as perfect and wonderful as any could have been.

I would be returning to Camp Pendleton, California for additional training and from there the future looked uncertain, so we decided to wait until my return to be married. We thought it was a wise choice and parted with all the usual tearful promises. Yet in the end I had a deep feeling that I should not leave her; that I shouldn't have joined the service; and that somehow our being apart was not going to be good for either of us. I shook off my foreboding thoughts as though things could never change between us...

* * * *

The campus at State vanished quickly and reality took its place as the uniformed Japanese conductor entered the car yelling in a high-pitched voice, "Shinn Garu! Shinn Garu!" He passed on through to the next car and I rubbed my eyes sleepily as I hoisted the seabag over my shoulder and headed for the door into another world.

Outside the station I hailed a taxi and directed the driver to take me to Camp. He teethed an amusing grin at me and said, "Campu Garus,OK, boss." It was several miles to the base and over some of the worst terrain I'd ever seen. I watched the little fellow as he drove the little car, and his regard for the trees and the corners seemed nil. The cab was small and cramped and I bounced from side to side, wondering if we were going to make it at all.

When we finally braked at the main gate, I didn't have to wonder any more about what the little guy had found so amusing. I shoved my orders out the rear window and the M.P. looked them over.

"You come in by train?" he queried.

"Yes. Just got off at Garu."

He laughed as he handed the envelope back to me. "They all get stuck with the same gag, so don't feel lonely; you could have taken that same train right on through to the Base. It stops up the street there." He looked up the road, pointing to a train station several hundred yards away.

"Thanks," I said, drawing my arm back inside. Then I turned back to the little Jap, who was crouched down slightly in the seat. "Listen, Buddy, get me to Division Headquarters! Now!" He wasn't grinning anymore and we drove on up the street, and darkness was settling in as we stopped in front of a long building with a large-lettered sign. "Headquarters, Third Marine Division, Japan."

Camp Garu had been a Japanese Kama Kazi base during World War II, and even after all these years its many scars and wounds were there to be seen. Large cement walls and bunkers had been torn up by bombs and were left where they lay, now scattered along the newly erected wire fencing. The former flyers' barracks had been made over to suit American servicemen and had been occupied by a small force of Army personnel up until the Korean War, whereupon the base became a steppingstone for training and supplies. It was now occupied by five-thousand Marines and about two-thousand Army personnel.

I had arrived one day earlier than necessary according to my orders, but decided I'd been sitting on my pants too long already and reported for duty. I was introduced to the personnel in the G-3 section, nearly fifteen men in all, and found myself settled down and working before I was aware of it.

My department consisted of an area near the center of the office. It had been marked off by three hard-board partitions and there were the usual drawing boards and paraphernalia that are familiar to a drafting room. The job of making maps and overlays for headquarters was one I had been trained for and was familiar with, and operating the little department quickly became routine. The only irritating trouble spot seemed to be my men. There were two of them – a Private named Dale, and Walt Eckbart, who was a Corporal. Dale kept calling Walt "Eyeballs". I had decided to stand my ground and learn a little before I shot off, but my irritation grew too fast and about the fifth time he repeated it, I couldn't constrain myself. I looked up at him and asked, "Dale, do you always refer to your superior as "Eyeballs?"

He stopped drawing and looked at me with a silly expression on his face, as though failing to discover for a moment whether or not I was joking. The expression and the fact that his glasses had slid half-way down his nose finally brought an unwanted grin to my face. Naturally, he took it the wrong way.

"Sarge, you mean to tell me that you've been here for two days and haven't heard of Rembrandt the Second yet? Look, I want you to meet the only man in the crotch who can make a map of Korea that will sell for five-thousand bucks!"

I looked at Walt candidly for the first time then. He sat there looking back, only he wasn't smiling one bit. He has a hooked nose that gave you the impression of staring into the face of an eagle, and he was looking at me with a set of eyes that could have belonged to Eddie Cantor, as they protruded somewhat from their sockets. Nearly twenty, I thought, and he isn't putting on any act. He peered at me as though expecting me either to break out with laughter or nod my approval. He certainly has an ugly kisser all right, I thought, but there's probably a hell of a lot more to him than meets the eye. I decided not to pass judgment at the moment and turned back to the overlay I was working on.

I had returned to the barracks from the mess hall and started to change the roll of film in the camera when my eagle flew over and perched on the edge of my bunk.

"Gonna take some pictures, Sarge?"

"No, at least not tonight...Just getting some of that damn sea-rust off. Don't tell me there's something around Camp Goofie, or Garu that is, to take pictures of?"

Walt grinned. "There are a few things of interest around...Depends on what you want to shoot, that's all." He thought a moment, then continued, "You'll have to take a look at my collection sometime. I've been here about two months and I've taken quite a few – mostly of my kids though."

"Your kids?" I interrupted, looking up.

He threw up an arm in a protective gesture. "Oh, they're not really my kids. I teach a class out at Garu Elementary School every Tuesday and Thursday afternoon. Didn't mean to startle you; I was referring to the children in the class." He finished with a hesitant look.

"Well, this is certainly a hot one! Just how did you manage a racket like that?" I finished putting film in the 35mm and wound it around as I listened.

"I applied for it right after I came here. There are two of us here at the camp doing it. We alternate back and forth. Guess headquarters thought it all up to help improve Japanese-American relations in the area, in particular for us servicemen. I think they were right and that it's a good idea, considering the lousy relations that existed when we first hit this Island…" he trailed off, hesitating again.

Wow, I thought, there must be better things to do around here than teaching school to a bunch of fat Jap kids who probably don't understand one word of English!

Realizing that I wanted to pursue the subject no further, Walt jumped up and promoted, "It's about a two-minute hop from here to the base pub. How about a beer, Sarge?"

"That's the first thing of interest you've had to say, Walt. I'll just take you up on that!" I shoved my hand out and he grabbed it, beaming like someone who had finally discovered a long-searched-for friend.

He was talking as he drank and I was thinking about that old saying, the one about all the artists being just a little bit off their rocker, and how he definitely fell right in line with it. Walt said he had been a commercial artist for an ad agency before the war, somewhere in upstate New Jersey. He admitted that it was hard to just sit and ink-in straight lines on maps all day, and that on occasion he had been throwing in a few flares of his own. The colonel over in G-2 had become extremely irritated one day at finding the main line of resistance located behind his own command post, and immediately had Walt's specification changed from draftsman to artist, hoping to get him a transfer. The transfer hadn't gone thru, however. "I guess Colonel O'Donnell has my bad reputation pretty well built up all over the base by now," he concluded, "but I haven't wound up in the can yet, so I guess I'm safe now."

"You're lucky O'Donnell didn't lock you up and swallow the key himself; you know that, don't you? If you'd have pulled a stunt like that in Korea you'd have been as liquidated as this glass of brew!" I drained the remainder of the beer from the glass and started to pour it full again.

"I see the situation around here all right," I admitted, "but what gives with you and this teaching bit? I can frame you as a screwball artist all right, but as a teacher, never. What's in it for you?"

Thoughtfully, he chewed the question over in his mind for a moment and then set his glass down. "I don't really know why I applied for the job. I guess I thought it would help occupy my time, but it's developed into something more than that now. Maybe you won't understand but here's how I see it. I didn't get any farther than high school and I guess I was nothing more than a desk number there. I never liked school anyway, but I managed to get through. Didn't make too many friends either, I suppose, and spent most of my spare time drawing and painting. Maybe it was just an inferiority complex now that I think of it. I've always had this thing that only my mother could love." He grinned wickedly as he pointed a finger at his nose. "The fact is, though, that for two hours a couple of days a week now I can stand up in front of a bunch of kids and have their complete and undivided attention. Don't get me wrong on that; I'm not power-drunk. It's just something I can't quite convey to someone else." He stopped suddenly and then said, "Here I go, babbling like some idiot! Shut me up when you've had enough, will ya, Gil?"

I picked up the glass and drank half the beer. "Well, it might be o.k. for you Walt but I could never see myself up in front of a group of kids like that! I'd make an ass of myself in no time. No Sir, not for me! You go ahead!"

"Ok, but it wouldn't hurt you to come along sometime and look on. You might..."

"No thanks!" I interrupted as I dropped the subject and finished the beer. If this screwball thought I was going to go watch him make a fool of himself in front of those little Jap kids, he was right out of his American mind! "Let's get back to the barracks. I want to get a letter off to Barbara tonight."

CHAPTER FOUR

"**S**ure glad you changed your mind, Gil. Bet you won't regret it." Walt's voice was drowned by the rattling of the jeep on the rough road.

"Changed my mind. Hell!" I shouted. "Just got tired of sitting around that damn base diddling with my maps! What I'm thinking is that here I am on my first liberty in Japan, and what am I doing? I'm going to some screwy class at a school…Hell, what I should be doing is seeing the town!"

"Better you should be going to this so-called screwy class than seeing what there is to see of town! Besides, I know what you'd do…go out to some bar and get plastered. Then you'd go lay some broad like the rest of the jerks do and come back busted and all screwed up! I wish more of 'em would take a visit like this instead. They'd be better off."

I thought about his remark but didn't answer right away. We were traveling through the countryside now. Everywhere were rice fields and everywhere in the fields were people: men, women and even children. They were all bent over, working and up to their knees in muddy water. I had the impression that I was seeing something as old and as ancient as Japan itself. Nowhere did I see a machine; instead, the people seemed to be the machinery and except for their methodic plodding through the rice paddies, they looked somewhat a permanent part of the landscape.

Now and then we slowed to pass two-wheel carts loaded with rice and I was aghast to see that nearly all of them were being pulled by women. After we had passed several of the heavily-laden carts, I nudged Walt. "Quite a set-up the men have over here. What do they do, marry a woman and make her their slave?"

He started to laugh and then saw that I was serious. "It's all difficult to explain, so I won't even try to give you a complete story. I doubt if I could anyway. It's simply a part of the life here in Japan. Call it custom or whatever you will, but the women seem to expect it, and as long as they aren't kicking, why should the men? That's a bit sketchy, I know, but when you've been here a while, you might see the light. I didn't get the drift right away either."

"Sure looks odd to me." I dropped the subject as we entered the edge of Garu. The town seemed big and as I looked, I mentally compared it with Lafayette, Indiana. This comparison was in size only, as population-wise I doubt if Lafayette would have had a chance. The streets were literally crawling with people of all shapes and sizes, all rushing about in short, quick steps that made the whole affair remind me of a walking race at the county fair. The street suddenly closed in on us and became narrow as the taller buildings rose alongside, and Walt had difficulty manipulating the jeep. He was laying on the horn and the crowd seemed to fall back in waves as we passed through.

The difference between the older and the younger generation was very apparent. The older people still clung to the long oriental garb, but the younger set, for the most part were sporting western style clothing. All of the people seemed to be fairly shorter than normal, and a statement that I had once read in a book on Japan flashed to mind. The author had stated rather matter-of-factly that the reason the Japanese people were short was a development of shorter legs. He said this was brought about over a period of time, and that it was caused by their continual squatting and sitting to do things that were normally accomplished by others in a standing position. If that statement is true, I wondered, then why are they so short from the legs up? I was about to tell Walt that I was rewriting history when a taxi-cab came up the street toward us. It looked for a moment as though it were going to slam into us but at the last second careened into a side street and disappeared. I was trying to see the driver, figuring it could have been only one fellow driving in such a manner--- the guy who had delivered me by air mail to Camp Garu that first night. Walt said bluntly, "They all drive like that – Worse than anything I ever saw in Jersey!"

After several more miles of dodging and weaving, we entered the suburbs and the narrow street turned into a much wider one. The stores and shops changed to low houses almost immediately and the crowds of people thinned out.

I had always thought that the Japanese lived in small paper shacks. These homes were quite the contrary. They were all quite large and had curved gable roofs that gave them a striking architectural appearance. They were nearly all bounded by high wooden fences, but now and then there was an open gate revealing a yard. There were large flower gardens in some of these yards and even sparkling fountains and miniature statues of Buddha and other shrines.

"You look surprised," Walt said, looking over at me.

"A little, yes. Not exactly the way I had it all pictured."

"Well, don't let it throw you. We're going through one of the better sections of town now. Most of the people living here are store owners and the like." He paused and then concluded, "The school isn't in a section like this."

He was right. Very shortly the houses became small and shabbier again and the paved street reverted to a rutted and unpaved one. Young children with dirty clothes and dirtier faces peered out at us from behind broken windows, and there were no gardens here, only now and then a small grove of trees where more children played.

The jeep lurched to a sudden halt and Walt jumped over the side. "We're here."

"Where?" I looked at the front of a building appearing to be no different than a larger home.

"The school, man! Where did you think, the Kasbah?"

I waved my hand. "I'd prefer Joe's bar! But this is a school?"

"Sure, come on." He picked up a package from the seat and I followed him through the door into a long corridor.

The building looked much more like a school now that we were inside. We walked through a corridor and past doorways leading into classrooms. From every room came the same sounds of children talking. It was remarkably like many of the schools in the United States, and even more so when we entered one of the rooms. It was empty of children, but I was amazed to see it full of desks and seats. Somehow I had always pictured Japanese school children as sitting around on the floor while they studied.

"You still look buffaloed." Walt walked over to the desk in front of the room and put the package down. "Take one of those chairs over there and be calm."

"Where's the kids?" I asked as I sat down.

"They'll be along in a few minutes. It's almost two o'clock now." He turned and started drawing on the blackboard. I was sitting there thinking about how much out of place I was when the bell rang. It was located on the wall directly over my head, and I made such a direct hit when I jumped up that I nearly put it and myself on the floor. Fire, I thought, as I started for the door! Then I heard the children laughing and talking as they poured into the hallway and I turned sheepishly. Walt was grinning from ear to ear as I sat down.

They filed in one by one and I simply sat and stared. They were all dressed in blue and white, and it appeared that they were wearing uniforms rather than normal clothing. The boys were dressed alike in blue trousers with white shirts, and the girls were wearing blue pleated jumpers with white blouses. Everyone of them was seated and looking straight ahead, and they all watched Walt as though he were the only person in the room. Not one of them had even looked my way and I had a sudden feeling that I did not even exist.

Walt suddenly turned from the board and said, "Good afternoon."

"Konetchewa," they all answered nearly in unison. They were smiling now and I looked at the blackboard, taking in the reason. Walt had drawn a picture – more of a cartoon than a work of art – and it simply showed a man extending a bone to a dog. The man sported a nose that was grotesquely long, and I realized as the children did that it was a caricature of Walt.

Walt pointed to his own nose and then to the picture. "I Walter. I feed dog." He smiled in a rather goofy way and the place erupted with laughter. I thought for a moment that they were laughing at him, and then suddenly I knew that this was not the case; that they instead laughed with him. I realized then why he had been unable to fully explain his reason for liking this job. He was a natural teacher. His ability to draw, as well as poke fun at himself, gave him a head start where the children were concerned, and the children were having fun while they were learning. What else could anyone hope for?

Walt suddenly stopped laughing and the children immediately stopped too, as though he had a string attached to each one of them. I supposed in a sense he did have. He pointed quickly to a little girl near the back of the room. "Now, Micheko, you say same thing."

The youngster stood up, never blinked an eye and said, "Walter-san feed dog."

Walt kept drawing more pictures, and this same process was repeated with other students. I watched with interest, in fact so intently that I did not immediately realize that someone else had entered the room.

When I finally saw her, she was standing just inside the door and looking around the room at the children. She was one of the most stunning women I had ever seen, and I was as amazed as it is perhaps possible to be. She wore a dress that looked as though she had just stepped in from a Fifth Avenue shop. Her delicately shaped face was accentuated by a petite, pointed chin. Her hair was swept back in a pony-tail. She suddenly glanced at me, and I guess I had my mouth hanging open in astonishment. She bowed slightly and smiled, then turned her eyes back to the children. I felt a little foolish as I forced my eyes back to the blackboard.

The bell finally rang and Walt waved his hand only once. The children filed out of the classroom, laughing and talking.

The girl walked over to Walt and smiled. "Walter-san, if you keep on you'll have them all spoiled. You know this is the only class where they're allowed to run wild. The one salvation is that it's also the only class where they may learn English. I will compliment you on that; however, I must add that I sometimes wonder about your devious and unorthodox methods!"

Walt laughed and answered, 'Thanks for the compliment, Toyoko." Then he turned and motioned toward me. "I want you to meet a friend of mine. This is Sergeant Gillaney. Gil, this is Toyoko Hiashitani, Principal of the school."

I felt my imagination slipping again as I walked over and extended my hand. This place was really full of surprises! "Very pleased to meet you, Miss Toyoko…Pardon me for looking surprised, but I'm afraid that I am!"

"Things over here aren't exactly what Gil thought they were," Walt spoke to Toyoko. "He came here with the same misconceptions we all did, but he'll come around!"

"It's not quite that bad," I faltered, "but I'll have to admit that I hardly expected to find all this."

Toyoko blushed slightly and I realized that I had been staring at her during this last statement. Boy, you're sure putting your foot in your mouth, Gillaney, I thought to myself. Better shut your trap before the rest of you goes in too!

Walt came to my rescue with, "Well, that should hold the little monsters for another week. We'd better get that jeep back to the base...O, I nearly forgot." He handed Toyoko the package that he had brought along. "Some candy for the kids. I didn't have time to pass it around. Maybe you'll be kind enough to do the honors."

"Thank you," she smiled politely. "I'll see to it that they get it tomorrow morning. But I still say you're going to have them all spoiled."

Walt headed for the door and I turned toward Toyoko. "I'm very pleased to have met you, Toyoko. Perhaps I'll see you again."

"You may come back anytime," she smiled.

I hesitated, risking a last disbelieving look at her and then turned to follow Walt through the doorway.

"So this is why you go running off to school a couple of times a week! With someone like her around I might even consider doing it myself." We were headed toward the base again, and the jeep was bouncing over the road unmercifully.

Walt smirked at me. "I know what you're thinking, old boy, but fasten your seat belt. She wouldn't even think of giving a uniform a tumble, and least of all me."

"How the hell does a beautiful creature like that rate scrounging around a shabby school? I've ogled at worse than her in the movies!"

"So have I, but the movie industry isn't very big over here," he laughed. "Besides, she's real well-educated, a smart cookie to you, and her father just happens to be the Mayor of this city. Make something out of that!"

"Why's she teaching in that dump?"

I received a dirty look from Walt and he was plainly irritated as he said, "I don't really think I'd call it a dump. Besides, her family lives here in Garu...Probably the only opening she could find in this area. And I wouldn't consider that being principal of a school was a disgrace!" He had me there and I decided I'd said too much already, so I watched the scenery go by as we approached the base.

CHAPTER FIVE

"**A**ll I know is that if things continue to progress in this fashion, half of the base will be locked up as dope addicts and the other half will be tailing one another around in suspicion."

Colonel O'Donnell was talking with General Donohu and I could hear them plainly through the thin Masonite partition.

"Well, we can't very well lock up the whole damn base," the General argued. "You know as well as I do what would happen. There are seven-thousand men here who are twelve thousand miles from home."

"Well, the Military Police are doing what they can, which incidentally doesn't seem to be much, and the C.I.D. is working on it day and night, and that isn't working out either. We've even held classes in self-protection. Nothing seems to stop the trend and I can see no other choice but to take more drastic measures!"

"Let's look at this thing a little more rationally, Colonel. Now I've asked for your advice, and mind you, I'm not saying that you're completely wrong…locking the gates could be the answer if it comes to that, but this dope traffic has just picked up recently. As you've already pointed out, the C.I.D. (Criminal Investigation Department) and the M.P.s are on the job, so I'm only saying that we should give them a little more time."

"All they manage to do is get leads on the little guys and pick them up," the Colonel interrupted. "Sure they lock up the users but under questioning the only admission I've heard so far is that they bought it from some guy on the street. All the little guys on the street look the same so where does that get you? The source of the stuff is what we really need!"

"Exactly, Colonel, and perhaps you may disagree with this, but I believe by locking up we never would find the source. It's an old story of sacrificing a few to save many, if you ask me. If no one buys, how do you find the source? Shutting down the base could possibly have some advantages, but I think they're over-shadowed by the advantages of leaving it open....for the moment, that is. However, if something doesn't break within the month, it may very well be necessary to do what you suggest." He paused a moment and then emphasized, "We sure as hell can't let the entire Third Division become addicts. You know as well as I do what's in store for this outfit in the near future, and I have no intentions of leaving Japan with a mess like this on my conscience."

That seemed to close the subject, for they began discussing some forthcoming maneuvers at Mt. Fuji. I tore my ear away from the partition and went back to the drawing board.

So that was what Walt had meant by his remark, 'Better you should go to this so-called screwy class than seeing what there is to see of town!' I concluded that he had probably been right.

That afternoon I flung my camera over my shoulder and jumped into the jeep. Walt looked a little surprised but said nothing until we were through the main gate and headed into the country. Finally he turned and remarked, "Thought you had enough last week, Gil. Fact is, I'd almost given up on you!"

"Well, I'm bringing my camera along this time. Thought I might get some shots of you and the kids whooping it up...you know, something I can show my own someday."

"By the way, Toyoko asked me about you Tuesday, wondering if you were coming back." He glanced at me out of the corner of his eye and grinned as I pretended I hadn't heard him. "Oh, I forgot. You're engaged, lovely and use nothing but the best makeup."

I laughed. "At least you're right about being engaged! And for Christ's sake, stop imagining things or you'll have that nose complex of yours rubbing off on me!"

The class had been in full swing for half an hour when my flashbulbs finally petered out. I picked up the collection of dead glass and walked out through the passageway leading to the playground in back. Some of the children were playing. I stopped and lit a cigarette as I watched them. They had a very funny way of skipping rope. Two girls were holding a long cord at either end and a third girl was in the center. This third member was not actually jumping the rope, nor was the rope turning, but she was more or less swinging her body gracefully over it.

"It's a wonderful game. It helps them to attain coordination and good balance."

Toyoko was standing beside me. She looked the same as she had before and beamed that automatic smile that had stuck in my memory. I tried not to stare at her but found it impossible.

"Good to see you again, Toyoko," I stated as I tossed the cigarette down and stepped on it. She said nothing, so I continued, "I took a few pictures of Walt and the kids. If they come out all right, I'll give you a set for the school."

"That will be nice. The children love to have their pictures taken. I'll put them up on the bulletin board for all to see."

For lack of words I continued, "I only hope they come out all right; I'm afraid I'm no pro at that sort of thing."

"I'm sure they will be OK," she smiled. "And I'm happy that you came back to see us again. I want you to feel free to visit the school any time you like. Perhaps you can even try taking over one of the classes some time; you can if you like, you know."

"I'd much rather leave that in Walt's capable hands," I asserted with a grin, "but thank you anyway."

"If you'll excuse me now, I must be getting back to the children. Good-bye." I said good-bye and watched her short footsteps as she disappeared through the archway into the building.

"We've arrived, old man!" Walt shouted over the never-ending roar of the jeep.

"What do you mean, 'arrived'? I thought we just left!"

"No, I mean we've really gotten there. We've been invited to a Cha-no-yu, or in good old American, a Japanese tea party."

"A tea party! What the deuce is that?"

"Sarge, old boy, I'm surprised at you! But if you really don't know, well, it's a special affair the Japanese have every so often to celebrate or commemorate something. Seems that Toyoko's father is throwing one for the teachers at the school, in honor of some fancy painting he's acquired. At any rate, she just invited both of us."

"And you actually accepted?"

"Sure, why not? I know it's rather a stuffed shirt affair, rituals and all that, but I wanna tell you that a real Japanese tea party is something very few Americans have ever been invited to. I'm going."

"Don't jump to conclusions, old boy! I didn't say I wasn't going. Where is this thing coming off?"

"Saturday evening at her father's house," Walt answered. "And don't be afraid. The other guests will wear kimonos or something, but Toyoko said we could wear anything we wanted to."

"Thank God for little green apples!" I shouted. "I just had a horrible vision of myself crawling around in one of those over-sized burlap bags!"

"Brother, have I got news for you," he grinned. "For your information those over-sized burlap bags are a hell of a lot more comfortable than what you and I are poured into now! They're not burlap, either; most of them are cotton or silk."

"Ok, professor, you've convinced me!" I interrupted. "Now do me a special favor, will you, and bring your mind back to this road and to those trees alongside that you're narrowly missing!"

CHAPTER SIX

We stood in the center of the garden and watched the Japanese guests. They were squatting around in separate groups and paid no attention to us as they partook in their own quiet discussions. They were all men and wearing dark kimonos and those ever-present wooden geta shoes that clattered loudly as they shifted from one foot to the other.

I glanced back at Walt. He looked totally unfamiliar in a suit. I had borrowed one from him and although it was a little tight it seemed pleasant to get out of uniform for a change.

"So where do we go from here, Walter-san?" The inference didn't alter him.

"We stay put until they notify us." He looked up and pointed to a bell hanging from a tree near the house. "That's the signal right there."

I shoved my hands into my pockets and leaned back against the cold statue of a lion. "You know a hell of a lot about this weird country for being here only a short time."

"I read books," he grinned. "You should try it sometime---at least try something besides blood and guts!"

"Well, this is certainly a lot of bunk! We could have just walked up to the front door and…"

"It's a custom they have," he interrupted, "and if you think this is queer, you haven't lived yet!"

He was right. Very shortly the bell rang out and I looked on in wonder as each of the guests walked over to the fountain, washed his hands and rinsed his mouth out with water. Then each, in turn proceeded to crouch down on his hands and knees and crawl through a small opening in the wall of the building. As our turn neared, I looked back at Walt.

"What in blazes is this bit all about?"

"Another custom: We're supposed to do this so we leave our pride outside when we enter the house." I was about to query, "What pride?" when he prodded me onward.

I kneeled down and crawled slowly through the opening, emerging into a brightly illuminated room. It was completely lacking of furniture and the only thing of note was a built-in alcove in one of the walls. In the center of the alcove hung a painting of an old woman who wore a weather-beaten face and was holding an armload of rice stalks. It reminded me of the thoughts I had had on my first ride through the Japanese countryside, and this woman seemed to be all the faces I had seen along the way, blended carefully into one. It was not a colorful painting; instead, it was one in a drab color that only added to its reality.

Each man ahead of me walked over, stood before the painting a moment, and then bowed. When my turn came up, I repeated the performance. I turned around then, making room for Walt, and sat down on the floor as the others had done.

When my eagle finally joined me and perched on the floor, I turned and whispered, "I've seen it all, brother! Now what happens?"

"We sit here quietly for a while," he whispered, "and then Hiashitani comes in and greets us."

"Is that it?"

"No, not quite. He serves each of us tea, and then we drink the tea while we admire his painting."

"Oh," I answered dumbly, "Not much of a tea party after all, just a quiet sort of old ladies sewing circle, you might say!"

"You might say it, but for God's sake, don't say it very loud. Some of these innocent-looking gentlemen speak and understand English as well as you or I do."

I whispered, "Well, you sure wouldn't have known it. I didn't see any of these little characters breaking their necks to speak to us out there in the garden."

Everyone stopped talking as a sliding paper door opened and in waddled our host. This, I thought, was what I had always pictured the Japanese man to be. He was a short, pudgy fellow with high cheek bones and graying hair. He wore a kimono of red silk, and as he waddled in he smiled broadly, exposing a set of rather large gold-capped teeth. He suddenly reminded me of some of the photos I had once seen in the travelogues of the fat Japanese emperor standing before his antique tea table. He walked directly over to Walt and bowed.

"So happy you could come, Walter-san."

"I'm very pleased to be here," Walt answered. "I think your new painting is very descriptive."

"I'm pleased to meet you, sir," I found myself saying. "I too think your new painting is nice."

"Thank you," he teethed, as he turned to the next guest. This greeting was repeated to each person as he met them, one by one, and I presumed that all of them were complimenting him on the painting as they would gesture to it now and then during brief exchanges of conversation.

Just as he finished making the rounds, and as though pre-planned, the panel from whence he had entered slid open again. This time it was Toyoko who entered. She was carrying a large tray of small cups and for a moment I hardly recognized her as the same woman I had met at the school. She wore a bright pink silk kimono with what appeared to be a large black bow tied at the back. There was just a trace of lipstick, but no other make-up to be seen. The sudden switch in her appearance made me feel out of place once more. She now appeared so native, whereas before I had looked upon her as being anything but Japanese. I watched with interest as she stood mutely looking down at her tray.

Mister Hiashitani suddenly took the tray from her and walked around the room again, presenting everyone with a cup of tea. Toyoko waited until last, then took a cup herself and sat down alone over in the corner by the door. As she sat and adjusted the long kimono, our eyes met for perhaps a split second, and I smiled. Her lips cracked slightly, and then just as suddenly they froze as she again looked downward.

"Why doesn't she sit with us?" I whispered to Walt.

"Another one of those unending customs," he answered. "And you can stop whispering now."

I looked around, and the other men were again talking in groups. "That's all, then?"

"Yup, the whole show. But we have to stay here a while; it would be considered rude to leave now."

"Huh!" I snorted. "They'd consider that rude! Now that's a joke. These men all appear to be teachers at the school and Toyoko just happens to be Principal of the joint, yet she's not supposed to mingle and talk or apparently do anything else for that matter? They must certainly have a cockeyed opinion of what's rude and what isn't."

"Hang on to your temper a minute, Gil. In the Japanese home the woman takes a back seat. Oh, she could be a wheel of some sort, a princess even, but once inside her father's house she's again his daughter, which means she is no different than any other Japanese woman. She might serve or even entertain, but she will not normally mingle with the guests – unless of course she happened to be the host herself."

"Oh, I see," I said, more to let the matter drop than for any other reason, for as I looked back at Toyoko, I did not see. She was still sitting alone, looking quite sober and a little dejected. Suddenly I felt an overpowering urge to see her smile and to see her laugh and enjoy herself. I wanted to get up and go to her. To hell with the stupid Japanese custom and tea party, I'd rather forget them both! I started to rise and Walt reached up, dragging me back to the mat. "Down, boy!"

I shoved my knees under me and looked back at her again. She apparently had noticed the action as she was smiling slightly as she stared down into her cup. "Well, at least she knows what I think of that stupid rule," I stated flatly.

"You keep this sort of thing up and you're going to win the first Japanese Oscar for unpopularity," Walt grinned as he rose slowly to his feet. "We'd better get out of here now; I think the party's breaking up."

Some of the men were going outside now. This time through the main door, and we followed quickly, saying good-bye to our host. I glanced over my shoulder toward Toyoko, but she did not look up as we stepped out into the garden.

CHAPTER SEVEN

The words just wouldn't come out and I finally threw the pen into the locker box and wadded up the paper. Hell, I thought, how many times does that make now? At least a dozen! I just can't write to Barbara. It's been almost a month now, and her letters still come in. But I can't answer them. Somehow it was different back home where we could talk easily to each other, but it isn't the same now. Why? She's still real, and so am I, and so is being here. What the hell! What would I say…"Dear Barbara – You'll never guess what I did the other day. I went to a real Japanese tea party! Can you fancy that?" What's the use, anyway!

I had been walking, and suddenly found myself at the main gate. I shoved my I.D. in front of the guard and walked on up the street toward the train station.

The Club First Chance was a dive near the center of Garu on the river. Anybody with an ounce of sense would have passed it by. I ignored the sudden angelic moralistic feeling, but I did wonder as I walked through the door how many men had found it to be their first and last chance as well.

There were no bar stools, but other than that it could have been any tavern in the States. There was a long bar with a full-length mirror hung behind it; the usual array of bottles and lurid pictures were present and about a dozen booths lined one wall. The place was well-baited for American servicemen. There was a small dance floor and an ancient juke box at the other end of the room. A private in uniform was doing a drunken exhibition of Arthur Murray to the tune of Buddy Morrow's *Freight Train*. He transfigured the train much more than the gentlemen he was imitating, but his buddy and their two Japanese girls at the near-by table weren't minding in the least.

The whole place reeked with heavy smoke and every booth and table was filled to capacity. The only exception was a table by the wall, where Sergeant Johnson sat slumped over a large bottle of Asahi beer, looking at nothing in particular. He was at least half-shot, but the only one in the place that I recognized, so I found myself sitting down across from him.

It was several moments before it registered on Johnson that I was present. When it finally did, he double-took me as though focusing his eyes. Then he jerked up, grinning.

"I know you. Yeah, I know you." He pointed a wavering finger in my general direction. "You're over in G-3. Gilford, or somethen…Ishen't it?"

"Gillaney," I corrected. "You're Johnson, from Photo-Repro Section, right?

"Thash right," his head nodded slightly from side to side. "I knew damn well I knew you! Well, tell me old man, how you doin'?"

"O.K. But I'm in bad need of a drink right now…how do I get one in all this confusion?"

He didn't answer me directly, but wavered to his feet and yelled toward the bar. "Hey Louie, bring my buddy here a beer!" The whole place must have heard him, and as he plopped back into the chair he smirked, "Hish name's probably Hero-Hito or shome other illustrious thing, but I call 'em Louie for short. Anyway, yer gonna' get yer beer!" The large bottle of Asahi beer was on the table in front of me before he finished talking, and I poured out a foaming glassful.

"Why the hell haven't I saw you in town?" Johnson queried suddenly. "You been here quite a while." His head wobbled again and then, "Oh, I get it…you been shacked up with some babe in town, I bet!" He laughed and nearly upset his beer as he swung his arm and slapped me on the shoulder. "Thash O.K.., buddy, I got me a babe here myself, so I understand."

I drank some of the beer. "Well, I don't exactly have a babe, as you put it. Fact is, I stay on the base most of the time…got a girl back home."

"For God's sake, man! You think thash any reason not to have shome fun? Lishen, I got a wife and two kids back home. I got me a gal in shpite of all that! She's the best damn thing since they invented beer. Got 'er in a house up the street aways, 'specting me home now, in fact!" He grinned rather wickedly.

There was nothing I could have said then that wouldn't have led to an argument, so I kept still and drank the beer. I watched him closely as he turned the glass over and over in his hand, and it was evident that his mind was wandering.

"This damn base," he finally said, more to himself than to me. "I wish the hell they'd send me back to the land of the 'mornin' calm'! I had shomethen worth-while over in Korea. I've been here for three lousy months now, surposed to be on R an' R. Ha! They call thish rest an recouperation!" He suddenly looked up at me. "Know shomethen? I got more damn enemies here than I had in the Chosen! My boys all think I'm a bastard, yes sir, a real bastard!" His voice fell off for a moment, then he looked at me soberly and asked, "You got troubles like that?"

"No, I've got ten men in my squad, but I don't believe they think of me that way---perhaps not even at all." I added hopefully, "At least not to my knowledge."

"You wanna know what, Gillaney?" He bounced his glass off the table and it was apparent that he meant business. "I'm lousy to those boys, an' I know it! I am a bastard! They don't like me even a teensy-weensy bit, an' I know it….I bet they hate my guts! Hell, I know they hate my guts! But those punks wouldn't lishen to my side, even if I made 'em I bet…You lishenen' to me?" It was a menacing look, and I nodded over the bottle. He had something to say, and it was more than apparent that he would be heard, so I listened.

"They think I'm rotten to 'em cause I'm rough on 'em," He shoved his thumb into his chest. "Well, I don't think I'm quite as bad as all that! I ain't one to make loushey excuses, but I think it's just this damn war. Mostly though, it was them young kids I had in Korea…the ones I saw get their guts blown out! Oh, sure, they was brave boys an' they fought hard, even died harder, I guess…but I'm tellen' ya that a little more trainin' and disciplinin' would've saved a hell of a pile of 'em!" He paused for a moment to catch his breath. "Now, I ask ya, jus' what good is the Medal of Honor if ya gotta die to get it?" He reflected a second and suddenly appeared to be quite sober as he added, "I jus' don't wanna see that happen to these kids, thash all; an' I only wish by Christ that they really knew how I felt the next time they point ta me and say 'There goes Sergeant Johnson, the son-of-a-bitch!'" He didn't bother with his glass then, but picked up the bottle instead and guzzled the beer first hand. It was evident that he was finished for the moment. I had heard of men who came back from battle with similar feelings, but to come face to face with one of them and really hear his unadulterated part of the story was suddenly a little frightening.

He jarred me loose from my thoughts as he slammed his bottle down again, only this time it missed the table entirely and blew into a hundred pieces on the floor. I peered at my watch. "It's almost midnight. Let's get out of here."

"Preshishly my feelings," he gurgled as he wobbled to his feet.

"Come on, I'll walk you to your shack." I supported him through the doorway, and he pointed up the street.

"Thish way, Gillaney." We stumbled nearly half a block, mostly on my feet, and we were passing an entrance to a building when a familiar form brushed by us. I looked up. Toyoko! I stopped to look, and she stopped to look at us. I started to speak, but Johnson beat me to it with "Hi ya baby! How about comin' along wish us?"

She turned almost frantically and without saying anything disappeared through the door. I looked up at the neon sign hanging over the portal. "Takoma Hotel. Now isn't this just great! What the hell will she think of me now?"

"Come on, Gillaney, over here!" Johnson was staggering through a doorway up the street, and I had a sudden urge to grab him and beat the hell out of him. However, his next performance may have saved his life – or mine. He uttered a drunken yelp as he missed the first step on the flight of stairs and fell flat on his face. I still wanted to hit the lug, but instead grabbed him under the armpits and dragged him to the top of the landing. A door slid open and a young Japanese girl literally flew out into the hall.

"Johnny-san, whats-matte-you?" It all came out in one syllable, which I had to decipher as she looked at me. "He stinko?"

"Yea," I growled. "He's stinko all right! Just ruined my whole evening too, the bastard!"

"Bas-ard?" she queried. I realized suddenly that she must know very little English, and felt relieved that she had not understood me.

"Nothing," I answered. "You take him inside now." I turned and started down the stairs and heard her yell "Sank you," as I entered the street below.

Once outside I walked back and stood in front of the hotel for a few minutes. "The first damn time I stick my nose off the base alone, and this has to happen!" I realized I had said it out loud for all to hear, and looked around. No one was on the street and I turned back toward the train station.

* * * *

Three days later I returned from the mess hall to find Walt sitting on the edge of my bunk, thumbing through some photographs. He had a grin on his face that increased in size as I came over. "What you been up to Walt? I haven't seen you around lately. You runnin' around with some geisha-girl?"

He laughed. "Not quite, but you're awful damn close…Look at these." He shoved the pictures at me and as I looked them over he told me the story. He had taken a trip down the coast to Takarazuka, where the famous troupe of Japanese entertainment women are located. He had watched a few of the stage shows and taken a few pictures on stage. What really amazed me was that the clown said he had actually crawled into their dressing room through a rear window and had taken pictures in there. And the pictures proved that he wasn't lying!

"I narrowly got out of there by the seat of my pants, and I'm not certain that the M.P.'s have stopped trying to match up the pants yet!" He concluded, "But believe me, they can lock me up for life; it was worth it!"

"I hardly thought you had the guts," I laughed. "The next time you decide to take a trip down there, you better plan on a passenger--- namely, me!"

"Sure Gil. By the way, I saw Toyoko on the street this afternoon."

"Oh, oh," I floundered, "here it comes!"

"I don't know what you mean; this should be good news for you. Anyway, she explained it to me. She's afraid you think that she's mad at you, if you can make sense out of that. She said it all happened Saturday night."

"Yea, it sure did. What a damn mess! What did she say?"

"Only that she watched you from her room and saw that you weren't drunk."

"Thank God," I breathed. "That damn Johnson was three sheets to the wind and I was helping him back to his shack…Sure looked bad!

"Well, I told you she was a pretty smart cookie, didn't I?"

Something came back to me with a start. "Wait a minute...what do you mean she watched me from her room? I thought she lived with her folks!"

"Not any more. The day after the tea party she had it out with her old man. Seems he's been planning an unknown wedding for her, at least unknown to her."

"She didn't know? How in hell does that happen?"

Walt explained. "It's another custom and the older people over here still go by it. The parents get together and plan the marriage before the two kids even meet each other. Anyway, she told her father she didn't want any part of it, so he ordered her out of the house. She took a room there at Takoma Hotel where you saw her. At any rate, I wouldn't worry about her."

"Who's worrying?" I found myself saying. "I wanted to see her some place besides that damn school of hers anyway, and I'd a hell-of-a-lot rather visit her at that hotel than at her old man's place!"

Walt looked suddenly thoughtful. "Yea, I suppose you're right at that. But take a little advice and take it easy, will ya Gil? I know a little about Toyoko, and she's not the type you just walk up to and grab."

"Now who's worrying? Perish the thought, pal. I'm a perfect gentleman!" I grinned as I walked over and flopped happily on the bunk.

CHAPTER EIGHT

The sign over the hotel entrance blinked intermittently as I stood and watched it for a few minutes, trying to gather courage. Suppose she doesn't like the idea of my coming here. Suppose she even throws me out on my ear. After all, this isn't something I really should do. On the other hand, she might be lonely and even appreciate a visitor. I finally convinced myself as I put out my cigarette and entered the building.

Walt had said that she had watched me from her window, so I went to the first door and rapped gently. There was no sound from within, but very quickly a man in slippered feet slid the screen open. He looked rather hesitant for a moment and then smiled, "Kombawa."

"Good evening," I answered, backing away. "I'm sorry to disturb you." He said something that I didn't understand as he slid the screen shut again, and I turned and walked up a flight of stairs near the wall. I passed several doors and rapped on the one at the end of the hallway.

"Just a minute, please." It was Toyoko. I fingered my cap nervously until she opened the door. "I saw you coming from the window, Gill-san. Won't you come in please?" She smiled spontaneously. She wore a dress this time instead of the kimono, looking much more like her natural self.

"Good evening, Toyoko."

She put her hand gently on my arm as I started to walk in. Please remove your shoes first."

I was embarrassed at not remembering this important custom, and she apparently sensed it. "At least I'm certain of one thing," she grinned. "You aren't accustomed to entering a Japanese girl's apartment!"

I laughed as I slipped off the G.I. shoes and stepped in. The room was small, about nine by twelve feet across, and at first glance there appeared to be nothing to it but a small, low table near the center with a few cushions scattered around it. Further inspection revealed a large vase sitting in the corner and there was a small window on that side of the room, facing the street.

"Please sit down." She gestured with her hand toward one of the cushions beside the table and I sat down.

Thinking some sort of explanation was in order, I said, "Walt told me that he talked to you yesterday, and I wanted to give you my side of the story."

She was still standing and cut in quickly. "You don't really have to explain to me; I was watching the whole thing from the window. You were only trying to help a friend."

"Friend, hell!" I looked up at her. "I've never even talked to that joker---at least not until that night! I was helping him home, all right. I doubt if he'd have made it by himself. He's shacked up with some gal about two doors from…." I stopped, realizing what I had said. She walked over to the wall, slid open a built-in panel, and reached for something inside. She didn't turn around and laughed rather heartily before she answered.

"Go ahead and say it. Such things are nothing new to me…it would be impossible to live here very long without realizing what's going on in town. Many of the servicemen keep girls here in Garu, and I suppose in some ways, it's even for the better. It could possibly help to keep the men out of more serious trouble."

It was the first time I had heard a defense of the situation and what made it even more surprising was that it was coming from a Japanese girl. "Come to think of it, Toyoko, you could be right about that…In fact, Johnson wasn't really in trouble; he knew exactly where he was going even though he was pie-eyed!"

"Pie-eyed?" she turned, looking confused for a moment.

"Drunk," I answered, "just slang for drunk."

"Oh." She looked at me as though about to say something else, but instead walked over and opened a screen leading to another room. "Would you care for some tea, Gill-san?" She hesitated at the doorway.

"I just ate about an hour ago, but if you're going to have some, then I will too." I stopped and shook my finger at her, grinning. "But, please, let's dispense with the ceremonies this time!"

She chuckled and her voice became hollow as she entered the other room. "I assume that it was your first attendance at a Japanese tea party?"

"My first and last," I answered, "if I have anything to say about it."

"You really didn't appear to be enjoying it much. I can't blame you for that. It's an old tradition here in Japan and there are many of them that I don't agree with, I suppose."

"Like marriage," I stated flatly.

There was a rattle as she dropped something on the tatami, and it was some time before she said anything. "I suppose Walter told you all about it?"

"Not too much, and it's really none of my business, but I sort of wondered what your side of it was."

"All right, but first come here and help me, will you please?"

"Sure." I jumped up and entered the other room, which was half-again as small as the first. She was bending over a gas burner near the wall while pouring water into a pan. There was a small table, somewhat similar to a card table, sitting in the corner. There were also two bamboo chairs.

"Would you take the table and chairs into the other room please; I'm afraid it's too small and uncomfortable in here."

I picked up the stuff and moved it. "This is more like it. I don't understand how some people can be comfortable sitting on the floor all the time."

"Enjoy them while you can," she answered from the other room. "I only have them for a week. I had to talk for an hour to get them from the hotel manager and they go back pretty soon."

"Why don't you buy some furniture?"

"Buy some? Did you forget that I'm a teacher? I have very little money saved. Everything I earned at home went to my father."

"That sounds like a raw deal."

"Oh, he gave me enough to buy the things I really needed, so it was all right." She came into the room with two steaming bowls of green tea and sat opposite me, then bent slightly to drink and as she did, her hair fell loosely over her shoulder. It was a beautiful jet-black and I was thinking how nice it would be to reach over and touch it when she straightened up. "You wanted to hear about a marriage contract?"

"Sure, go ahead." I watched her features change as she talked, and it was almost as though she were acting, although I figured she wasn't.

"First of all, let me say that my father is not such a bad man. Instead, I'd say that he is quite typical of the present-day businessman. He is the Mayor of the City of Garu, and he is constantly scrutinized by the public, of which there are two kinds: Those who lean toward the western style of living, and those who still favor the old ways. He's a well-educated man and is quite aware that pleasing all is impossible. Still, it's his duty to try. This is not easy, especially since he has the never-ending government policies to contend with plus many complex local problems. Anyway, one of those old customs is still strictly adhered to, and it is marriage." She sipped on the tea before continuing. "The Mayor over in Nagoya City and my father have been very close since childhood. He has a son. I have never so much as talked to this young man, and I see no reason why I should marry him---other than to please two old friends. So, seeing no logic to it, I refused. It's all as simple as that. Hereafter, I am no longer considered to be a member of my father's household...and that, however, is not so simple." She paused as she swallowed heavily and I saw tears forming in her eyes. "I still love my father and mother very much. My mother somewhat agrees with me; still she cannot question the law of my father."

"But where do you go from here? You can't live like this forever---at least, not easily!"

She didn't look up. "I've given that a lot of thought in the past few days. It wouldn't be right for me to stay here in Garu much longer. Things of this nature get around very fast and it would not be good for either me or my family. I'll probably go to some other city to work."

"Where could you go?" I started to light a cigarette and she went over and took an ashtray from the open panel. As she put it down in front of me, she said, "I've read of the scarcity of teachers in the United States, and I can tell you that no such condition exists here in Japan. There are more teachers here than are necessary. I may have some trouble locating another position, but I'm certainly not afraid to try." She was blinking as she looked down, and I reached over and laid my hand over hers. It was the first time I had touched her, and she felt warm and soft.

"Let's go somewhere." I looked at her squarely as she slowly raised her head.

"Where?"

"Oh, I don't know. They've got movies here, haven't they? I forgot, though; it probably wouldn't be good for you if we were seen together. Probably just give people something else to hit you with."

"Since I'm going to move, it really doesn't matter and I would like to see something other than the inside of a school building." The place looked brighter as her eyes began to shine. "There's a Kabuki theatre just a short walk from here. We could go there, and if you don't understand it, perhaps I can explain it to you. It's very interesting."

I rose quickly and pulled her up by the hand. O.K., Kazookie or whatever it is, here we come!"

CHAPTER NINE

Walking into that Kabuki theatre was somewhat like returning to some Shakespearian era. We passed through a matted corridor decorated with colored lanterns and an usher met us inside the theatre. Toyoko paused and whispered to him in Japanese. He said nothing in return but simply kept wagging his head up and down. We were then led up a narrow flight of stairs and into a box. I tapped her on the shoulder. "Why don't we sit below?"

She turned and smiled rather apologetically. "I thought you would rather stand up and watch. These boxes are especially for people who would rather not sit below on the floor."

"You're serious?"

"Really. I asked the usher to bring us here."

I nodded approval and the usher finally bowed out, leaving us alone. We walked to the edge of the box and looked down at the narrow, curtained stage. At the moment it was dimly lit by several torches. No one was in the center but two men were seated along one side of the curtain. One of them was chanting from a book while the other was playing an instrument that from a distance looked like a mandolin. It had a rather twanging sound as though it were out of tune. I recognized it as the same instrument I'd been hearing on the radio in the barracks.

Looking down at the sea of black heads in the audience, the people seemed to be divided into groups, sitting and squatting in individual sections. Toyoko notice my perplexed expression.

"They seat the people that way more or less in family groups. In fact, the whole family usually comes together to see the show."

"Oh, now I get it." I looked on with interest as a woman with a baby strapped to her back shuffled her way up on aisle and turned into one of the stalls. She apparently found her home for she squatted down. I turned to Toyoko. "Are we too early for the show?"

"Early?" she giggled slightly, as she looked at me in amusement. "No. This is just a short intermission. The show started at noon – we're about to see the last act."

"The last act!" I repeated as I glanced at my watch. "It's nearly ten o'clock!"

"I forgot to tell you, these shows run all afternoon and evening, nearly eleven hours," she explained quickly.

"What about the actors? They must be nearly dead by the end of the day!"

"They have many actors, not just a few. They rest during the intermission anyway."

"What are we going to watch?" I asked.

"The name of it in English is *The Forty-Seven Ronin*," she replied. "It is the story of a man who kills another man in the emperor's palace. He is punished by death…."

She stopped suddenly as a man in bright costume wandered slowly onto the stage from the left wing. He uttered a few words that were somewhat like a chant. Another man entered behind him from the other side. I could swear that cold-blooded murder was being performed before my very eyes! The second man drew a short knife from a fold in his kimono and promptly thrust it into the back of the other. I looked on, unable to speak as the man who had been stabbed died a thousand times. He writhed and chanted something terrible, and I could even see the blood gushing from his back!

I found myself unable to tear my eyes away from that stage, and as the show progressed, I never once had the feeling that it was an act. In fact, it was the greatest display of murder, mayhem and mutilation imaginable!

The fellow who had so skillfully performed the murder was quickly captured by several guards and immediately beheaded. Now several new actors entered the scene. They crawled into a castle through a rear window and threatened what appeared to be a lord with long samurai swords. After several minutes of loud, intense arguing, the intruders assassinated him. They were immediately captured by the castle guards and were taken before a court for trial. After more loud chanting and wailing, each prisoner in turn took out a knife and committee hari-kari. The upshot of the whole thing was that they were all put to rest in a hillside.

The stage was still full of actors, but the show appeared to be over so I turned to Toyoko. "It is rather funny, isn't it?"

Her face was streaked with tears! "Funny?" She choked out as she looked at me in disgust. Then just as suddenly she turned sorrowful again and she said slowly, looking down at the stage, "It's very sad…very sad."

I stood dumbly, finding no means to convey the desire to make up for my stupidity. I didn't recall just when I had taken her by the hand, but I clutched it several times as though this might tell her that I was sorry. She seemed so delicate and defenseless, I suddenly realized how much she meant to me. Something was happening and I felt it churning in the back of my mind, telling me that I had been through all of this before. I realized what it was then when a fleeting picture of Barbara flashed before my eyes, but I blinked it away quickly as the curtain fell on the stage.

We were carried out with the crowd and Toyoko was silent as we walked slowly up the street. The play had plainly aroused her emotions, so I decided to let the conversation lag.

At the end of the street we passed under a large half-moon shaped arch. I broke the silence to ask her what it was.

"A Torii. We're entering a Shinto shrine." She seemed to reflect for a time as we walked up a cobbled pathway and long rows of bushes. Finally she said, "I came here with my family many times when I was a young girl."

"Is Shinto your religion?"

"It was." She paused and we sat down on a wooden bench facing a large, circular fountain. "I have no real religion now. You might say that I'm caught in the center of things where religion is concerned. My family is still loyal to the faith but since going away to school I have lost contact with it." I watched her carefully as she spoke and was pleased that she had chosen me to talk to. "So I cannot say that I am Shinto, although I wish I could. In fact, the type of religion one has no longer seems of consequence to me, only the fact that one believes in something or someone. Believing in something or someone gives a person courage to carry out ideas and plans. It becomes something that is lived every day, not just one or two days a week, so which faith one actually belongs to is unimportant."

She stopped short as she must have realized the effect her words had upon me, and to put it rather mildly, I was flabbergasted. Here was a woman who seemed to be totally unprejudiced. She could reason and make decisions with startling quickness...and to think that I had once told myself that all Japanese women were short, fat and very common! She was anything but that. Impulsively and without warning, I turned on the bench and drew her to me. The kiss was gentle and she did not draw away, but she did not respond either. I drew back, searching her eyes, but she said nothing and looked downward.

"Toyoko, I've wanted to do that since the first moment I saw you... You must have noticed that before now."

"Yes, I have noticed. But getting involved with you wouldn't be right, even if I wanted to. It would only make matters worse."

"But do you want to?"

"I think we should go," she said softly as she rose from the bench.

We walked quietly, hand in hand, back up the path and down the street. As we drew near the Hotel, I pulled her gently into a store alcove and kissed her again. As we stood there our bodies seemed to mold together as I pressed her to me tightly. This time she returned the kiss passionately for just a moment; then freeing herself quickly she backed away. The neon sign overhead revealed tears glistening on her cheeks as she whispered, "Good night, Gill-san." Turning, she walked slowly into the hotel. I watched the doorway several moments after she had gone. How I wanted desperately to run after her, to hold her again...

I stood by the moonlit window, slipping off my shoes, when Walt groped his way over in the darkness. "Where the hell you been, Gil?" His foot collided with the locker-box that was partially protruding from under the bunk, and he uttered a yelp as he fell.

"Damn! You hurt?"

"No."

"Well, be careful. You'll wake up the whole barracks!"

He perched himself on the locker and repeated, "Where've you been?"

"Why? You writing a book?"

"For God's sake, no! But apparently you haven't heard the news yet. General Donohu's orders are out for the M.P.'s to pick up any G.I.'s wandering around off base after midnight. You just got in under the wire. I was worried, that's all!"

"Well, on top of everything else this is just great! Man, I'm really batting a thousand tonight."

"What da'ya mean by that? You been to see Toy?"

"Yes," I stated simply.

"I thought so. You're stuck on her, aren't you?"

"Seems to me you're getting awful damn personal all of a sudden. Besides, you started the whole thing, don't forget that!"

"I'm not forgetting, and maybe that's why I'm getting awful "damn personal", as you put it! Anyway, what are you going to do now?"

"I don't know – nothing, I guess. But she's really got me…like being hit with a ton of bricks. I'm worried, Walt." I paused as I thought of what had happened tonight. "I really wanted to have that woman tonight. Guess I'm lucky she had some sense; otherwise, I might have…" I paused and then said, "Besides, there's still Barbara."

"Anything I can do to help?" He stated it earnestly, but the sudden thought that I was confiding in him made me swell with anger.

"Yes. You can go back to bed and mind your own damn business!" It had a terrible sound to it, and looking over at him quickly, I said, "I didn't really mean that, Walt. I'm confused, that's all."

His eyes brightened in the waning light. "Well, you know what they say, 'When in danger or in doubt, run in circles, scream and shout!'" He laughed and I damn near reached out and hit him.

"It isn't funny! Now get the hell back where you belong; I want to think!"

"O.K., you'll feel better tomorrow," he muttered as he withdrew to the other side of the barracks.

I leaned back against the pillow and soon fell asleep.

CHAPTER TEN

The Colonel's voice was still ringing in my ears after the formation had broken up and we walked back to the barracks.

"Sergeant Earnest James Johnson, for illegal use and possession of narcotics, sentenced to ten years at hard labor in the federal penitentiary, forfeiture of all pay and privileges, and to be thereafter reduced to the rank of Private…"

That was always the way it was, making an example of somebody in order to scare hell out of the peons! I'd like just once to hear them read one about some officer! And now it's Johnson. Hell, I never thought that he…"

"Sort of hitting close to home, isn't it?" Walt was walking alongside and brought me back to reality.

We entered the barracks and stretched out on our bunks. Lighting a cigarette, I said, "Not exactly close to home, but it sure took me by surprise!"

"I thought so. Your face hit your spit-shine when the Colonel read it. Johnson, he's the guy that almost nixed you and Toy, isn't he?"

"Yes, that's him all right. But that's not the worst part of the deal. He's got a girl in town. I'll bet she doesn't even know anything's happened! Hell, she'll probably rot there in that dingy little room, waiting for him!"

"She will if she loves him and doesn't know what's happened."

"She didn't act as though she hated his guts that night I saw her." I stopped, remembering what Private Harris had said aboard ship when we were entering the harbor: "The first thing I'm gonna do when I get off this trap, is head for Tokyo. I got a gal there that's been cryin' her eyes out for me nearly three years!" I'd hated him for what he had said then, and now I realized for the first time what he had really been talking about. "I'm going to see her tonight. If she doesn't know the score, then I'll tell her."

"You feel better now than you did last night?" Walt's voice was quizzical, not knowing if I would talk or tell him to go to hell.

"Well, maybe I could sort of fill you in on a few of the details. For one thing, Toy's decided to move away from Garu. She says she can get another job and she thinks it's the best thing to do."

"You gonna let her do it?"

"Gonna let her do it? Hell, what else can I do...marry her myself, I suppose, and send her to the States?" It was out before I fully realized what I was saying, and when it hit home I froze. Marry her! What a joke! Even if I wanted to, she'd probably laugh in my face. Besides, it's a stupid thing to even think about. She's nice, but....

"Well, you can't just stand on your hands and stack bee-bees on a pool table! Marrying her wouldn't be such a bad idea at that. You could do a helluva lot worse!"

"Sure, I could do a lot of things, but I've got another world waiting for me back in the States. I can see myself introducing my new Japanese bride to my family. I've seen others come back and try that. Some of them, if they were lucky, got as far as the door! That's all!"

"I know you better than that, Gil, and I know a little about Toyoko too. She'd fit in as though she were made to order for the job. It wouldn't be long before those doors would open up."

He had a point, all right, but I wasn't ready to listen so I laughed as I jumped up

and began changing into my civvies. "Boy, what a cupid you are today. You thinking of starting a lonely-hearts club?"

"No." He refused to see anything funny.

"Want to come along?"

"No, it's your show. Besides, I have something else to do tonight. Good luck, anyway." He turned and walked back to his bunk and I finished putting on my trousers.

I climbed the narrow wooden stairway and knocked gently on the edge of the shoji screen. Several moments passed and I was nearly ready to give up when padded footsteps approached on the inside. Then the screen slid open. Chiako stood framed in the doorway. She looked as though she hadn't slept for several days; the black rings around her eyes seemed to off-set the jet-black hair askew on her head. She stood for a time before recognizing me, and then when she did, she feigned a weak smile. "You know Johnny-san. Come in, please."

I slipped off my shoes and stepped inside. The room was a shambles. There were papers and magazines lying all over the tatami mat, and loose odds and ends were strewn about as though she had simply dropped everything where she might have finished with it. As though she had read my mind, she looked around the tiny room and said softly, "I---not feel bery'well."

"You know about Johnny?"

Her eyes came back to mine for a moment. "Hi, I hear. I bery sorry him---I rove him too much."

Her inability to pronounce certain letters in English made it difficult for me to follow her words quickly, but it was different and quite pleasant to listen to. I suddenly had visions of her and Johnny sitting together and talking in this sort of Pidgin-English, as they must have done many times. My attention slowly wandered and it was she who kept the conversation going.

"Johnny-san is no more. I try to go work---forget, I bery good at make clothes…"

"You need money?"

She smiled slightly then and said, "Johnny give me tock-san okani---I have too much now. Sank you." She paused again, thinking to herself. Then, "I tell Johnny you help him, las-a-week. He jus' raugh and say he no remember. He good man most of time, but I can-no understand him sometime…" Her voice trailed off as she turned toward the wall.

I leaned against the door jamb and lit a cigarette. Then the idea of bringing up dope entered my mind. It had apparently already entered hers as again she beat me to the punch. "Johnny use dope now, maybe two, three months. I not know first, but I find out soon…I try tell him this no good, but he jus raugh---he all time raugh. We bery happy together."

Before I realized it, I blurted out, "Where did he get the dope?"

She turned around quickly and looked me full in the face. "I can-no tell you… Besides, I not know anyway!" The last part had been more of an after-thought, as though she had not been thinking clearly at first. "Prease, you go now. Sank you for come see me…I not forget." She walked over and slid open the screen and I followed her. I slipped into my shoes and looked up to say good-bye, but she had already closed the screen behind me.

As I walked up the street to the Hotel, I felt a slight touch of anger. The sound of her voice when she had said, "I can-no tell you," had been more like "I would tell somebody, but certainly not you!" I wondered why. She doesn't know me! Johnson hardly knew me, either. The only time I had ever so much as talked to him had been that night. Hell! I'm imagining things now.

I knocked and there was no answer so I slid the screen aside and peered in. The room was the same as the first time I had seen it, and Toyoko was not there. I walked downstairs and into the street again, and I had gone a few steps when a familiar form caught my eye. As I turned, looking down the street, Walt walked through the door leading to Johnson's apartment! My feet were glued in place for a moment as I tried to reason. My mind might have been in an imaginary state or a quandary before, but this was no trick. Walt didn't know Johnson---at least he said he didn't...Hold everything; he could be looking for me. I told him I was going to see the girl! I was about to head over there when someone grabbed me by the arm.

"Gill-san. You wait here long?" Toyoko was smiling at me.

"No. Just got here," I lied, as I looked down at a sack she carried. "What kind of goodies you got there?"

She shoved it at me laughingly. "For your information, nosey, I've been buying something to eat, and if you're going to join me, you can carry it!" I grabbed her arm and we continued upstairs and into her room.

I watched her set two places at the small tea table, and was about to sit down on a cushion to wait when I smelled a familiar odor. "What's cooking?"

She answered from the kitchen. "The name is Su-no-mano." It's a sea food."

I walked over and stood for a moment, watching her put strips of fish into a pan of boiling water. "You should see the way we fix them back in Michigan. First, we catch a trout. That's the first secret – we have to catch one, and then we clean them. We leave the heads on though. Then we roll 'em in flour and cracker crumbs and put 'em into a pan with some butter, and WOW!" I patted my stomach and she turned around grinning.

"This is a slightly different method. However, if you like, I'll leave them raw."

"Raw! I'll have your life if you do!" I grabbed her around the waist as I stood behind her. "O.K. I'll have them your way! Now, how do you fix them?"

"Well, first I'll put them in water to boil for a few minutes. Once they're done, I'll steep them in vinegar. They're good with Saki."

I'd heard quite a few of the men tell about getting drunk on this Saki, but I hadn't tasted it so I decided to show my ignorance. "I've heard that's pretty potent stuff. What is it, anyway?"

She shot me a little look of wonder, as though she were certain I was fooling, but smiled and said. "It's wine, made from rice. We make nearly everything from rice here in Japan. Anyway, it's served while warm and if you're not careful, it'll get you stinko!"

"I don't care. Matter of fact, I think I want to get stinko!" I was still holding her waist tightly, and as she turned, our eyes met. We did not speak as our lips found each other. The kiss seemed unending, and I had a feeling it might last forever. Finally she drew back, but our eyes remained in contact as she remarked, trying to ward off the emotion, "It will be ready in a moment. There are some cards inside the fusuma, if you'd care to entertain yourself while you're waiting."

"Fusuma? Where's that?"

"The cupboard in the other room. I'm sorry, but I keep forgetting my English."

I straightened up and looked down on her again. "Toyoko, you don't have to apologize for what you say or do, not to me." I turned and walked into the other room, feeling her eyes on the back of my neck until I was out of view.

The meal was excellent and the Saki was beginning to make me glow with warmth. It was wonderful sitting across from her and exchanging conversation, and I found myself wishing she were the only one in the world to talk to or be with. Suddenly there was no other woman, only her, and I wanted to hold her close and tell her so, to love her and to make her happy.

She hadn't turned on any lights and there was just the glow from the hotel sign outside the window. I propped one of the cushions against the wall and leaned back, looking at her longingly. "Come here Toyoko… Please." Silently she slid around the tea table, laid her head on my shoulder and I began to stroke her hair. It felt silky and very soft as I ran my fingers through it slowly. Suddenly she trembled and looked up at me. "Gill-san, I can't understand my own feelings. When we were at the shrine, the first time you kissed me, I wanted to hold you then just as now…Something told me 'no'. I've seen many Japanese girls with American men, but all this time I've said to myself that it must never happen to me. I've told myself that it is not good….but that was all before I met you, and I do not feel that way anymore."

"Toyoko, you know how I've felt since the first. I don't think I've hidden it very well. In fact, I haven't really tried." I paused as I gathered courage from within, and the Saki must have helped a little. "I must confess that I've been trying to fight it too. You see, Toy, there is a girl back home. Barbara. We've been engaged for over a year now. We met in college. She was everything to me then. She seems so far away right now, as though she never really existed at all."

"Gil." It was the first time she had dropped the "san" from my name and it sounded good. "You and I are here in Japan and you must forgive me for this, but I see things a little differently now. For me, there shouldn't be a yesterday, no Barbara, nor a tomorrow. Just today. It's an old Japanese philosophy but one I completely agree with. And I have you here now, today…" Her eyes were like liquid fire, burning into mine in the gathering darkness. "I do not care what you did before or what you may even do again. I care that you and I are together now…right here…" She stopped as my mouth closed over hers. We locked into an embrace and slowly slid down until we were lying on the mat. With a long and passionate sigh, her hand slowly slid down and she began removing her skirt. We remained kissing as I gently helped her take the remaining undergarments off and then slipped out of my clothes. Then, as though the moment would slip away forever if we did not hurry, our bodies became one in a series of frenzied movements. There, on a rice tatami in the strange country of Japan, I knew for the first time the true meaning of complete love…

CHAPTER ELEVEN

It was nearing eleven o'clock and we had been sleeping several hours when I awoke and checked my watch.

I was almost dressed when I stumbled in the darkness and Toyoko sat up with a start. "Gil! Where are you going?"

"I've got to get back to the base. New orders. Everyone has to be on base by midnight. Stupid rule! A few jerks ruin it for everybody."

She arose and took a kimono from the fusuma. As she put it on, she asked softly but quite seriously, "Are you angry with me, Gil?"

I grasped her again and kissed her long and hard. "Now, would I do that if I were mad? I love you, Toy, and I feel about you as I never have about anyone before."

Her eyes glistened with tears in the semi-darkness. "Gil, I love you now, and I know that I will always want to love you this way…there's just one thing…" Her voice faded away softly.

"What's that?" I finished buttoning my shirt and looked at her again.

"I want you to come to me and to love me, but we cannot stay here." She paused as she wrung her hands nervously. "We'll have to find another place, if you really want to."

"If I want to? You bet your sweet little heart I want to. I'll look for a place for us tomorrow night."

"No!" She interrupted me strongly. "I can find a place easier, I think. Besides, if you try, they will make you pay too much. No, I can do it much easier." She paused again. "I really wish we could stay here in this place, but I think you can understand. My family would soon find out and I don't want to do anything to hurt them."

"It's the only thing we can do, Toy. I think I can understand your feelings and I'm certainly not anxious to cause you or your family any trouble."

I kissed her again and started to go. Then I remembered and stopped. "How the dickens will I know where to find you?"

She thought a moment and then said, "Walt will be at school tomorrow, so I'll write the address down and give it to him."

"Well, now, how about that. Good looks, love and smarts all rolled into one!"

As I turned and walked out, she looked after me. "You've heard the old American saying, 'it takes one to know one!'" I laughed and felt exceptionally warm and good inside as I walked down the stairway and hailed a taxi in the street.

Barbara had been the farthest thing from my mind for several days. I had not written a letter to her for over a month and I had not received one in three weeks. The thought of her came unexpectedly in the morning, along with a small package in the mail. I tore it open and there was the ring. Her mother had sent it and there was a letter attached.

> *Dear Gil,*
>
> *Barbara does not want to send the ring to you or to write to you either, so I'll do the best I can. I don't really know how to say it properly.*
>
> *Since you have been gone, she has changed and I'm really sorry and ashamed to have to tell you. She has been going with another man now, and I'm afraid they're going to get married. You know how much I've always thought of you and that is what makes this so difficult for me. You would eventually find out anyway, and it might hurt you more later, so I felt it my duty to at least try and explain.*
>
> *I hope you will still remain a friend of the family when you...*

I discontinued reading, wadded the letter up and tossed it at the trash can. I recall no feeling of remorse as I put the ring on the shelf of the wall locker and closed the door.

"Here...Toyoko says you're expecting it." Walt shoved the envelope at me and sat down on the foot locker. It was sealed and I tore it open.

"Dear Gil, Please give this to a taxi-driver and tell him to bring you to this address..." The rest was in Japanese script and I couldn't read it.

54

She had signed at the bottom, "Hurry to me, I love you. Toyoko." I stuck it in my shirt pocket and replaced it with a smoke.

"What's the big secret? You two planning your own private war?"

I had forgotten that Walt was there for the moment and I looked up quickly. "Yea. I'm B.O. Plenty and she's Dick Tracy, and we're trackin' down that unfamiliar odor...and right now I'm pretty close to it!"

"O.K., wise guy," he interrupted, "I just thought you might let a buddy in on it. She handed it to me with all the secrecy of the high command, as though it were a crypto or something!"

"Good girl," I mused. He appeared irritated and it made me think about seeing him the night before. "So you think we're playing games, eh? Well, what about you?"

"What about me?" He said it simply and I watched the expression on his face. He appeared indifferent so I took a different tact.

"Since you're getting nosey, old man, I'll do the same...What did you do last night? Hell, I'll bet you were playing detective and following me. For all I know, you could have been outside our door, listening for those little cries of passion..." I smiled as I let my voice drop and watched him. He wasn't squirming.

"Don't be silly! I went to a show last night. What the hell do you think I am, anyway, a peeping tom?" His voice was a little high, and his answer rattled me. I tried not to show it but I suddenly had the urge to reach out and grab him and ask why in hell he'd gone to Johnson's apartment. Somehow I couldn't, so I got up instead and started taking off my clothes.

"No, I don't think you're a peeping tom, little boy. Now get the hell out of here; I'm gonna take a shower!"

"All right, Gil," he turned toward his bunk. "But keep me posted. I'm a part-time justice of the peace you know, in case you two really get serious!"

I feigned a smile and said, "Ok, I'll remember." I left him standing there and headed for the shower.

* * * *

"Sure you want this address, boss? Maybe I take you to nice prace, many girl, good time...eh?"

He was the joker who had first brought me into camp and there was no maybe about it this time. He had turned and was teething at me as we drove down the narrow street.

"No, dammit! You take me to that address, you hear. I'll break your little yellow neck if you don't!"

He said no more and drove on. We passed the Takoma Hotel and the Club First Chance, then turned into an alley across from the Shinto shrine. Near the center of the second block the cab stopped and he pointed to a place across the street. "Here, boss. Please, you pay one hundred-fifty yen." I paid the little robber and got out, watching the cab until it had disappeared around a corner.

I stood there a moment and looked at the house. It was two stories with an arched, grey blue tile roof. The side facing me looked drab and old and I looked closely for an entrance of some sort. Dammit, the way they build a place over here, you can't even tell where the door is! I was still searching with my eyes when a section slid open. Toyoko stood and motioned to me with her hand.

"Gill-san! I've been waiting for you." I stepped inside and slipped off my shoes as she slid the screen shut behind me.

"There are two apartments here. An old woman lives down here; we have the upstairs. You don't mind, do you?" She looked apprehensive.

"Do I mind? I'd stay anywhere with you, Toy!" I picked her up and carried her to the top of the stairs. She laughed all the way up and when I put her down, I kissed her soundly. "Where do we go from here?"

She slid aside the shoji screen and when I looked inside the room, I was startled. It was much larger than her hotel room had been and there was a table and some chairs near a wall. A large arm chair and a foot rest sat in a corner, and a picture hung on another wall. I looked back at Toy and she was smiling. "Do you like it, Gil? I've worked all evening to..."

"Well, sure I like it, but..."

She interrupted me as she slid open another screen. "Wait, there's more!" I walked over and looked in. There was a real bed complete with pillows and spread and even a small dresser! I turned to her in astonishment.

"This is wonderful, but where...?"

"I didn't do anything rash, Gil. These all belonged to a girl I knew. Her boyfriend just returned to the States last night and she's going back to her home in Yokohama now, so she has no use for them. I bought them from her very cheap…Do you like it?" she repeated.

I grabbed her and kissed her again. "This is just like old-home week! Wonderful!"

"I want you to be happy here. Very much so, Gil!" She was standing by the bed, looking more lovely than ever.

"I am going to be very happy here, Toy. We're both going to be happy." I picked her up again and this time I lowered her gently onto the bed. She looked up at me and reached out her arms. I stared down at her for a short moment and then fell onto the bed with her.

CHAPTER TWELVE

To say the least, we were two people very deeply in love. The fact that Toyoko was Japanese and I an American seldom occurred to us, and when it occasionally did, it was of little consequence.

I sat in the chair listening to the music on the radio I had bought at the PX. Although there was very little popular American music broadcast, we often sat in the living room or lay in the bedroom and listened. The strange flute and violin melodies were somehow relaxing and I found myself beginning to like it.

"Gil, have you ever taken a bath?"

I broke up with laughter and she looked at me furiously. "I mean a Japanese-style bath!"

Still laughing, I answered, "No, Toy, I haven't, but I've taken many showers. In fact, I take a shower every night before I come here to you." I stopped laughing and forced seriousness. "I'll try anything once."

"I'll go get it ready," she said as she got up from the cushion. "It's downstairs. I asked mama-san if we could use it and she said it was all right."

She took my kimono from the fusuma and held it out to me. "Please get ready. I'll be back in a few minutes." I grabbed it and stole a kiss as she tried to get by me.

"Do Japanese women really scrub their husband's back?" I was smiling into her face and she knew I was joking, thank the Lord.

"History books don't often lie," she grinned and wrinkled up her nose. "However, if you don't want me to, I won't. In fact, I may even get nasty and pour cold water down your back when you're not looking."

I was about to say, "Down the back, eh, another old Japanese custom?" but I caught myself just in time. Instead, I said, "As long as it's you, I won't mind."

She disappeared down the stairs and I began undressing. She had surprised me with the kimono the night before. It was beautifully made of raw silk, and she had the seamstress monogram G I L in large letters near the front pocket. I finished putting it on and sat down. I thought how wonderful it was, just being here with her.

It wasn't really very large or even an exceptionally nice place, but to us, so completely engrossed in our love, it had become a heaven on earth. I had given her back the money she had paid for the furniture and told her that I would pay for the apartment.

"Gill-san," she was yelling from the bottom of the stairway. "It's ready; come on down!"

I padded down the stairs and looked down the narrow hallway. At the end was a tile square set into the floor. She had taken off her kimono and was climbing over the side of the tub when I came up.

"Isn't it pretty small?" I asked.

"No, I'm not sitting down now, I'm standing up. It's quite deep." She stood almost to her waist and her wet bronze body shown back at me. "Come on, get in," she laughed. "It's nice and warm."

"Both of us?"

"Of course. There's plenty of room. We can even sit down. There are stools over there to put on the bottom." She motioned to several wooden stools sitting alongside. "Hand them to me."

I gave them to her and she put them on the bottom of the bathtub. "See, I can sit down now." I crawled over the side and sat down facing her. The water was warm and felt good.

"Did you haul all this hot water yourself?"

"No, silly. There is a little gas heater underneath a tank beyond that wall. It heats very fast. I filled it with a hose."

"Oh," I said. "Where's the soap?" She turned around and took a bar of perfumed soap from a little shelf.

"Here, you want to wash your hair?"

"That's what I'm here for." I took it and washed my hair and she dried it with a towel.

"Now turn around and I'll wash your back, smart guy!" she laughed.

59

"O.K., I've always wanted to have my own personal back washer." I turned around and she washed my back. She even took a soft scrub brush and scrubbed it for me. "Boy, I've never had a rub-down like this one! Not even after a football game."

"Football? Did you play football, Gil?"

"I played in high school and a year in college. It was a lot of fun," I reflected. The athletic director nearly had a hemorrhage when I told him I was leaving for the service."

"You must have been very good." She was rubbing my neck and shoulders and I glowed warm inside.

"I've seen a hell-of-a-lot better…I'll probably go back and play again when this Korean thing is over. I don't know now."

"You won't have to go to Korea, will you?" She stopped rubbing and I turned around, looking into her worried eyes. "Toy, there's nothing I want more than to stay here with you, but I'm a Marine and we can't forget that. Whenever and wherever my outfit goes, I'll have to go too."

"I hope it isn't soon," she said as she began washing her hair as I watched her.

"It will be quite a while yet. I'm not sure, of course, but that's what I've heard."

"I hope it's a long, long time." She finished her hair and I helped her dry it. When she pushed it back again and looked at me, her eyes were a little red and she said, "Gil, I don't want to think about that time coming, not ever…"

I reached out and pulled her to me. We stood in the water and as our bodies touched, we once again felt that magnetic desire for each other. Our love was overwhelming; it didn't matter where we were or what we were doing, we were only aware that our love for each other was overpowering. There was no struggle or thought other than love as we held each other tightly there in the water.

* * * *

There was an empty lot facing the bedroom window. There were a few trees and bushes, and in the evenings Toy and I would often lie on the bed, watching the children play there.

One night I noticed that the lot was quiet and that the trees had been removed. Instead, there were now four very tall bamboo poles erected in a square in the center, and there were long ropes tied from pole to pole with bits of torn white paper attached.

"What's happening?"

Toyoko looked out the window and answered my question. "They're going to build a new house," she said simply.

"But why the poles and the paper and all that?"

"You have no way of knowing, so I'll try my best to explain it to you. It isn't very easy to understand, but I remember we did the same thing when my father built our house." She peered out the window, obviously reflecting as she talked. "It has to do with the religion of the man building the house. He is Shinto. In Shinto temples there are stretched woven rice ropes with those pieces of paper attached. They call it Gohei, an offering to the God. According to legend, a long time ago Amaterasu, the Sun Goddess, disappeared. The Shinto priests hung strips of cloth from the sakaki, sacred tree, and in this way they lured the Goddess back. It is now considered a necessary sacramental thing to do to ensure a bright and happy home."

I listened with interest as she talked and wondered how much more there was to learn about this strange country. I had not long to wait.

The next evening I looked out again and noticed that a small podium or stand had been set up in the center of the lot. There were people standing around solemnly and a man was stepping onto the platform. As I watched, he took out a book and began chanting. It was short, and when he finished, he picked up a tree branch, shaking it up and down three times.

Toyoko watched with interest until it was over and the lot emptied. Finally she said, "That was a ceremony to please the gods. Now the work on the house will start."

"You mean they go through all of this before even building a house? Hell, back home we just pour a foundation and start to work!"

She turned to me and sighed softly, "I did not think you would understand. It's something you have to grow up with – another custom, I'm afraid."

"Well, it sounds all right, I suppose. Is that all there is to it now? Do they build the house and move in, or is there more of this stuff to contend with?"

"I'm afraid there is one more thing," she laughed. "They still have the "mun-age" to go through, but that's really the best part of all."

"What's it all about? You've got me hanging now, so don't stop." I put my arm around her, watching her as she explained.

"Well, once they have the framework of the house done, they have a ceremony to raise the ridge pole---you know, the one in the center at the top." I nodded. "They gather together at nightfall, all of the men who are building the house. The owner brings Saki and everyone gets pretty stinko. Anyway, if they're able to by then, they erect the ridge pole. Sometimes they put it up beforehand, but they still have the party. I believe it's done to show the appreciation of the owner toward the builders."

"We have almost the same ritual back home," I reflected. "I remember once when I helped my brother move. He brought along a case of beer, and after the work was done, we had a real beer bust!"

"Beer bust?" she queried.

"An old American custom," I grinned. "It means everyone gets stinko and has a hell of a good time. It all amounts to the same thing."

"I'll bet there are a good many things quite common between Japanese and Americans, if people would only take the trouble to learn. That always seems to be the problem...ignorance..." Her voice trailed off and I kissed her in the moonlight.

"You and I aren't very different, are we?" I asked.

She did not answer me, but clutched my hand as we lay in the semi-darkness. I had been thinking of telling her about Barbara and the ring, but it suddenly seemed unnecessary. I had what I wanted now and at this moment the past was something I was willing to forget.

CHAPTER THIRTEEN

The midnight curfew ended as suddenly as it had begun. Word got out that it had been an absolute failure. General Donohu had been right after all. The only thing they managed to do was drive the men undercover. When midnight approached, instead of coming to the base a good many of them were staying in some hotel or bordello, and the military police were unable to break into those establishments.

I was sitting at the drawing board and sketching an impromptu cartoon when Colonel O'Donnell stomped in. He muttered to himself, thumped into his chair and grabbed the phone.

"What is this damned place coming to anyway! Operator! This is Colonel O'Donnell...O'Donnell! I wanna talk with Major Vette in Criminal Investigation....that's right!" There was a pause and then, "Hello, Vette? What in hell you doing over there, sitting on your ass? You heard me! I just read the morning report and they picked up three more boys last night! Listen, we've got to get something about these jokers pretty soon or you and I are going to be pushing pencils back State-side!" He listened a moment and then continued, "Yea, well I don't doubt it; he just skated up the middle of my back too!...Well, you know what I've maintained right along: lock up the whole joint---Donohu still disagrees so we've got to work something out...O.K. sit tight. I'll be right over!"

He banged the phone on the receiver and got up. I was still looking at him and as our eyes met, he glowered menacingly. I turned back to the drawing and he stomped on by and out the door.

"Personally, I think it's about time he got off his dead butt!" scowled Walt. He too had been listening and turned around facing me.

"Careful. Talk like that will get you a shaved head. Besides, they'll get it ironed out."

"Yea, they might…now that he's decided to play Indian for a while instead of Chief!"

"I've always thought O'Donnell was a pretty good guy, but you're carrying a chip, Walt. What did he ever do to you?"

He turned back to his work and said over his shoulder, "Nothing in particular; I just don't like him."

Walt was not his usual self. I tapped my pencil on the drawing board as I pondered that thought. He and I had seemed to hit it off good at the start, but the past few weeks had somehow changed him. His jovial attitude no longer seemed to exist. He stayed around the base very little now. The few times we had met were usually when I came back from town late at night, and then when I had tried to start up a conversation he somehow managed to avoid it. There still was no explanation for that night when he had gone into Johnson's apartment. I had wondered about that too, but had decided not to bring it up. After all, there probably was a logical reason for it and everything else. There usually was. The fleeting thought that Walt might be on dope himself had even crossed my mind, but that too was pushed aside as my better judgment told me to forget such an insane idea.

That evening Toyoko was not at the house. I looked frantically for a note, but there was none, and a quick search of the place revealed nothing. I turned and walked back into the street. It was unusual that she hadn't left a note or somehow gotten word to me. Maybe she had been detained at the school. After all, a situation like that could arise easily. I shoved my hands into my pockets and walked the three blocks to the Club First Chance.

The place was nearly deserted and I was feeling no pain when the guy came around from behind the bar and stood beside the table.

"Prease, you go now. I crose for night. Prease." I looked up at his smiling teeth and then down at my watch. "My God, nearly one o'clock! I must be drunk enough to swim!"

He helped me to my feet and when I had made it, I pushed him back. He nearly fell over a chair, but recovered in time and backed away from me with one hand up. "So-sorry; prease, no trouble. Just you go now, prease."

"Please! So Sorry! Christ, don't you Japanese know anything else? All right, I'll go…What I'd really like is to push your Goddamn smiling teeth down your throat!"

A sudden anger had taken hold of me. I couldn't control it, and I took a wild swing at him. I must have been at least six feet away, and my feet went out from under me. The floor came up quickly then and the lights disappeared.

My whole body ached and my head seemed to spin in a crazy circle as I tried to focus my eyes. When the room finally stopped moving, I looked around. I was lying on a blanket on the floor and the place seemed familiar. I started to get up when Johnson's girl walked into the room. "Gill-san! You O.K. now?" She reached down and lifted on my arm as I wobbled to my feet.

"How in hell did I get here? What time is it anyway?" I caught my breath as I realized it was Saturday and I didn't have to be back on the base.

"Nearly noon. You sleep a long time." She stood in her kimono and watched me as I took out a cigarette and fumbled for my lighter. "You pretty stinko last night!"

"I know…I know, but what am I doing here?" Then the thought occurred to me that Toyoko was probably waiting for me and worrying. "I've gotta get out of here."

"I watch you in bar long time. You try to fight…"

"I remember; damn stupid of me," I interrupted. "Guess I really made an ass of myself."

Mr. Kasi-chan own bar…he not mad at you, help bring you here." She paused a moment then, "I not know where take you but here. You no mind?"

I forced a smile. "No, I didn't really have much choice anyway and I must thank you Miss….What the hell is your name anyway?" I faltered, "You never did tell me."

"Chieako," she said and she smiled then. "I fix something for when you wake up. One moment prease."

She walked into another room and I tried to get my bearings. What would Toyoko think of me now? Gil, old man, you've really flipped your old wazoo this time! Better get over there and explain now…I started for the door as Chieako came back into the room.

"Gill-san, wait prease! I fix coffee." The thought of a hot cup of coffee stopped me cold and I smiled as I turned around.

"You Japanese women seem to think of everything, thank God. I never knew you drank coffee though." She handed me a cup and motioned for me to sit down on the little rice bag I had just used as a pillow.

"Not often drink coffee...cost too much okani. This Johnny-san leave with me. He buy P.X." She had sat down on a cushion and was sipping coffee as she looked deep in thought for a moment. "He buy many things at P.X."

"You miss Johnny a lot don't you?" I queried.

"Yes...I try forget, but is not easy. He very good man until..." she stopped for a second and then dropped the bomb on me, "until he start use dope. That's why I want you stay, have coffee; I want you hear me."

"What is it?" I had the feeling she was going to tell me something that I didn't want to hear, but I listened expectantly as she continued.

"I think all last night, not sleep. It is hard for me to say to you...I know about you and Toyoko-san."

"Toyoko? What's she got to do with it?"

"Nothing" – it sounded more like "nosink," and she paused a moment. "Toy bery nice---I know her many year. But Mr. Hiashitani, he not so nice I sink..."

"Her father? What the hell are you telling me. That...."

"Maybe I not tell you. Can cause much trouble for you..." She looked away.

"Listen, Chieako," I grabbed her by the arm. "You say it! If you know something, you tell me, hear! Don't you worry about me. I want to know!"

I let her go and she drew back for a minute before she spoke. "One night Johnny....he come. He too stinko an' not know what he say or do. He give himself shot with needle...heroin I sink, an' I fight with him. I ask him why...why use." Tears were rolling down her cheeks and she wiped her eyes. "He bery mad me...swear bad, an' then he say Mr. Hiashitani name. That all, no more...but Johnny-san cry then." She paused, "I neber see him cry---bery sad..."

I stood up and paced over to the window and back. "What the hell, that doesn't prove anything; maybe it was a coincidence!" But I knew even before it was out that it didn't just happen. There had to be more, and I puffed earnestly as I thought. Now that would be a stupid thing... The mayor of a city like this a fence for dope? Never! But if that hadn't been what Johnny meant, then what? Suddenly I stopped pacing and turned around as my mind clicked.

"Now, you tell me something, Chieako." I pointed with my finger and it roamed nervously. "You remember the night I came here to tell you Johnny had been arrested. Well, somebody else came here right after I did! What did he want?"

Her eyes dried and she thought a second. "I forget man...Man did come."

"What did he want? Did he tell you his name?" I waited impatiently for her answer.

"No, no name....just he ask you here. I tell him you just go, he sank me and go then."

"That's all?"

"That's all, I sink."

So it had to be Walt and he had been looking for me, but why didn't he come to the hotel; he knew I'd be there. Could be that he didn't want to disturb us, but then why did he lie? He knows Mr. Hiashitani quite well...

I thanked Chieako for the coffee and information and hurried out. The cold fall wind hit me full in the face as I walked down the street and the headache had disappeared by the time I reached the apartment.

CHAPTER FOURTEEN

Toyoko met me with a yell as I reached the top of the stairway.

"Gill-san! Where have you been?"

I pushed on by her and into the room without taking off my shoes. "Drunk, that's where…getting dead drunk!"

"Look at your clothes! Get them off now; I'll fix bath water," she paused and turned around near the door. "We'll talk later; you don't look very well."

"I feel all right. I ought to, I've slept all morning," I interrupted her with a growl.

"You change and I'll fix the bath." She peered at me briefly and then disappeared down the stairs. I turned around and took off my clothes, flinging them onto the bed through the open shoji screen.

The water was so warm and relaxing I nearly fell asleep. She was rubbing my shoulders and neck and brought me around with, "I waited for you last night, Gil. I was very worried…You've never done that before.

"I came here last night," I interrupted. "You weren't here so I went down to the club for a beer." I found myself explaining to her even though I had previously decided not too; I continued anyway. "That beer must have been several or more, I guess. At any rate, I had no intention of getting plastered."

"I was not here because of a teachers meeting at the school; surely you must have realized that."

"Oh, I thought of that. I just wanted to get a beer and think, that's all. The more I thought, the more I drank and I guess I finally stopped thinking and kept right on drinking." I stopped for a moment and then lied, "Anyway, I woke up a little while ago in the back room of the club."

"I'm sorry, Gil. I didn't have time to get word here to you, but I wish that you had waited."

Somehow my bitterness had oozed away a little and I smiled at her and said, "Next time I'll wait!"

The thought of the curfew dawned on me and I grabbed her and kissed her lightly. "Guess what!"

"What?" She motioned for me to get up and as I did she rubbed me briskly with a towel.

"The General's decided to stop this 12 o'clock business. We can stay here all night now." I waited for some pleasant reaction, but there was none. Instead, she stopped and stared at the towel for a moment. When she did speak, it was faltering.

"I have to talk with you, Gil. Let's go back upstairs and then I'll tell you something." Her voice dropped and she headed for the stairway.

I stood in astonishment for a moment and then followed her. She sat at the table with her chin in her hands as I slipped into the kimono and sat down.

"Now what the hell is this all about? I thought you'd be pleased."

She reached over and put her hand over mine before she answered. "I would like to stay with you every night, all night, but..."

"Well, what's the matter then?"

"The meeting last night, at the school," she faltered slightly but no tears came. "They have a new principal now; I am through there."

She did not look up and I reached over and lifted her chin. "You mean you're canned? Fired?"

"It's all right. I was going to leave soon anyway, you know that."

"Yes, but there's still no reason! Did they give you one?"

"No, only that there had been a private meeting of the Board. I wasn't invited to attend. They don't have to give a reason anyway."

"Several things could have happened," she reflected realistically. "You and I could have been seen together, that is very possible, or..." she stopped suddenly and her eyes turned away.

"Or what?"

"My father."

"Your father!" I shouted. I was about to say 'he's always cropping up'. but thought in time and changed it to, "He couldn't do anything like that, could he? Even if he could, a girl's own father wouldn't..."

69

"My father, you forget, is still Mayor of this city and he carries a lot of influence. I'm afraid he doesn't think much of me now anyway, and if by chance he has seen us together or has ever been told that we…"

"Well, I'll be a son-of-a-bitch," I yelled as I pushed away from the table, upsetting my chair. "One fine old man you've got, I'd say! And just what the hell does he have against American men anyway? Compared to these scrawny little Japs, we're…"

"I don't think he has anything against Americans personally," she interrupted, "although he was an officer back in the war."

"Well, what is he doing, still fighting the war? Or maybe he doesn't know it's over! Could be someone should remind him of that! Putting all that aside, you're still his daughter!"

She looked squarely at me then and said, "That's just it; I'm not his daughter."

I had to fight for self-composure as I sat back down.

"I'm an adopted child. I've known it for some time – ever since I knew enough to check my birth records in Tokyo. I did that while I was in college. My parents aren't even aware that I know it, and they've never told me." She paused briefly and then continued as I listened to her unbelievingly. "My mother was Japanese but my father was a French Ambassador. It's all in the records. I was adopted when I was two years old. I never knew."

I was up pacing back and forth as she continued. "At any rate it's all simple now. I'll have to move and get another job in some other city."

:Like hell you will!" I stopped pacing and pulled her up to me. "You're gonna stay right here with me! I make plenty of money, don't worry about that…"

"It isn't a question of money." Her head was lying on my shoulder and her words came in my ear. "I have to go. Perhaps it may sound foolish to you, but I still love my family very much. They were the only thing that I've ever really known outside of teaching. They've raised me and helped me in many ways. My father even paid for my education. It's funny now that the only thing I can do to repay them is to leave them."

I held her out at arm's length and looked at her then. "Suppose I told you that your so-called father isn't really such a principled and devoted man. Suppose I told you that he is, and believe me now I really think he is, right up to his neck in vice!"

I realized suddenly that I shouldn't have said it.

She broke away from me and walked over to the window. She looked out, but I could tell that she wasn't really seeing anything. Her voice tearfully cracked and a little anger showed at the same time.

"By what right do you say this, Gil? I've known you only a little while, and I've known my father for a long time. This thing you say; are you angry with him, or is there something definite that you know?"

I realize that she was absolutely right. I didn't know anything for sure, except what an emotional Japanese girl had told me. As far as disliking Hiashitani, even hating him, and for sure I had every reason to do this, particularly after he had thrown Toyoko from her home, the reality of the situation made me suddenly want to take back what I had said. Damn anger, anyway---it seems to cause half the trouble on earth!

I came up behind her and wrapped my arms around her waist. "Toy, I'm afraid I've said something I didn't mean to say. It's just that I heard a rumor…"

"A rumor! You base a statement like that on rumor? I had thought of you as being much less impetuous!"

"Sure, I'm impetuous, but if I am, you've made me that way." I kissed her gently on the ear. "You know how I feel about your father's throwing you out---I love you, and I naturally dislike him, so when I heard…"

"Then you're not certain," she interrupted, and her voice seemed to calm slightly. "What I want to know is who told you this."

I should have anticipated that question, but I hadn't and before I thought I blurted out "Johnny Johnson's girlfriend!"

She broke away and walked back to the table. "I knew her back in school…Chieako. Did Johnny tell her this?"

"She said he did, when he was drunk one night. They got into an argument. He had been trying to give himself a shot of heroin, and she had been trying to stop him."

"I don't think Chieako is capable of lying, whatever else she may do, but this is very hard for me to accept." Her voice became barely a whisper and she walked slowly toward the kitchen. "I must think about this. I'll fix something for you to eat. I'm afraid I'm not very hungry." Her voice trailed away as she disappeared through the door.

CHAPTER FIFTEEN

The backyard was no more as the new house was nearly completed. The workmen were going in and out with arm loads of finishing and plumbing supplies, and inside, the hum of a saw ran constantly. I sat on the edge of the bed and leaned out, watching as I thought to myself.

It had been a foolish thing to blow my top about Mr. Hiashitani, particularly to Toyoko. She had taken it well, considering I had practically called her father a crook, even if he should be. What else could Johnson have meant? And this feeling about Walt. What if he did tie in somewhere? What the hell! I'm in this thing up to my ears now; I might as well find out.

"Toyoko, I have to go back to the base for a while." She had been doing dishes in the kitchen and yelled from there.

"Why? I thought we could stay here tonight."

"We can. I'll come back; I just want to see somebody."

She appeared at the bedroom door then. "Gil, you're not going to the Military Police, are you?" She looked suddenly tired and drawn as though she had been worrying.

I walked over and kissed her gently on the forehead and said, "No, it's nothing like that." I had never told her of my suspicions about Walt, and to do so now would only make matters worse. "I just want to check over a few records of my own. I have an idea, but I'm not too certain of it yet – suppose I tell you about it when I come back?"

She looked down, forced a smile and then looked up at me again. "All right, Gil. But please don't start any trouble now…promise me!"

"I can assure you of this," I cupped her chin in my hands, "what I'm going to do has nothing to do with your father, and I have no intentions of going to the police about anything, even though I probably should... at least not now."

She kissed me, and as I looked down upon the face of the one I had grown to love so much, I wondered if I had just told her the truth. For a fleeting moment the thought of staying with her was overpowering. Then I shook it off and put on my shoes. I left her worried, shaken form and walked out the door.

Walt was not in the barracks and I went over to Private Dale's bunk. He was lying there thumbing through a magazine.

"You see Walt around lately?"

He looked up with his usually foolish grin. "Oh, hello there, Admiral."

"Where's Walt?" I repeated. "You seen him lately?"

"Yes, as a matter of fact, I saw all of him lately. Just this morning in the shower....!

"You idiot," I interrupted, "you're about as serious as a penny arcade! How in hell did a guy like you get in the service anyway?"

"Oh, it was easy," he smiled. "The sign said 'Join up now and climb the ladder', and I thought it was the Fire Department!"

I turned around and started to walk away. His voice changed. "Well, if you're that damn serious about it, he was here just a while ago..."

"Where did he go?" I spun around, facing him again.

"Christ, you are serious, aren't you?" He swung his feet over the side of the bed and sat up. "Well, he came in tossing his camera around. I think he was out taking pictures."

"A logical conclusion," I smirked, "but where is he now?"

"Hell, Sarge, I'm getting around to it if you'll give me time!" He stood up and lit a cigarette while I waited anxiously. "Well, after he takes pictures he usually goes over to the Service Club and develops them. They've got a darkroom fixed up over there and he likes to finish them." I didn't wait to hear him finish as I rushed out of the door.

There was an empty dance floor and a bar over in one corner where several men sat playing cards. I glanced at the various doors across the room. One of them had a sign which read "Music Room," another read "Library", and the one on the end said "Darkroom." I walked across the floor and opened the door quietly. A light was on and negatives hung

73

drying on clips attached to lines that stretched from wall to wall. A print dryer hummed on a small table in the center. There was another doorway across the room with a black curtain hanging across it. I walked over, lifted it gently aside, and stepped in, drawing it closed behind me.

Inside hung the usual second curtain, used to insure total darkness at all times. I waited a moment as my eyes adjusted to the darkness, and then pushed it aside just enough to look in.

The room was small, and a form stood over a section of the full-length table against the wall. The dim red light hung overhead, and Walt was agitating a print in the developer tray with a pair of tongs. As I watched, he held it up to the light, shook it gently over the tray and then dropped it into the next one. As he did, he turned slightly and then stopped as though he had suddenly had the suspicion that he was being watched. He turned his head around and looked me full in the face. He caught his breath and swallowed at the same time, and his already protruding eyes seemed to nearly leave their sockets as his head jerked backward. Then at about the same instant, he tried to recover, faltering as he did so.

"Gil! What are you doing here?" He forced a smile as I walked over under the light beside him. Still looking directly into his eyes, I reached in the pan with my right hand and fingered for the picture. I hadn't answered and he grabbed my wrist as he spoke again. "Careful, that stuff there is potent. You'll get burned."

I located the photograph and pulled it out as I said definitely, "I know Walt; I worked in one of these dark little cubby holes for a few months back in school."

He stepped backward a pace and stood dumbly then as I held the picture up to the light. My eyes left his face for the first time as I examined the print. It was an enlargement of two men walking side by side leaving a building, and would have been normal except for one thing---one of them was Hiashitani.

I dropped it back into the fix and looked at him again. "All right, Walt, I've strung along enough now. What the hell is this all about?"

He stood motionless as he shot back, "What do you mean, it's just a picture, isn't it?"

"It's a picture all right, but just between you and me, I think there's a hell of a lot more to it than that!"

"Meaning?" He looked a little more concerned now as he spoke.

"You know darn well what I mean. I'll bet you're right up to your nose in trouble, and I'd like…" I was nearly shouting and he stopped me with a wave of his hand.

"For Christ's sake, take it easy a minute, will you. We'll go out in the other room and I'll…"

"Take it easy, hell! I've got darned-good reason to believe that your buddy there in that tray is …"

CHAPTER SIXTEEN

"Shut up now, and that's an order!" The words echoed at me and I stopped breathing for a moment before I answered.

"What do you mean an order?" I breathed out slowly. He looked at me squarely and said softly. "Just what I said. An order." He stopped for a moment, then watched me as he continued. "Now, let's go out into the other room and I'll explain." He reached into the tray and took out the picture, looked at it for a second, and then dropped it into the hypo-tank before he brushed by me and on into the drying room. I followed him numbly and blinked several times as the bright lights struck me again.

I watched him cautiously as he reached into his pocket, took out a pack of cigarettes and slowly and with deliberation lit one. As he did, I realized that it was the first time I had ever seen him smoke. He inhaled deeply several times and then sat down on the edge of the table, not looking at me. He did not even appear to be the Walt that I knew then.

"Gil, you're forcing me to do something that I wasn't ready to do yet, at least not until the job was completed."

I hardly breathed as I waited, and when it came I nearly lost my balance.

"You're into this thing now as deep as I am, I'm afraid. You see, I'm not really who you think---Oh, I'm Walt all right, Lieutenant Walter Eckbart, to be exact."

He saw my dazed expression and continued quickly, "I've been working on this dope thing ever since I came to Japan. I'm a member of the Criminal Investigation Department, the C.I.D. Nobody, not even the

General of this base knows this, with the exception of you now...I wanted you to know soon, but not yet."

"My God," I breathed, "you mean that all this time you've been in the outfit and nobody knows?"

"The C.I.D. here isn't even aware of it yet. I've been strictly on my own, until now, that is." He pulled on the cigarette and I sat quietly, losing all sense of feeling. "I've known right along that if things worked out, you would be helping me, but I didn't plan on it so early."

"What do you mean 'helping' you?"

"I wanted you to get to know Toyoko...and this is a hell of a thing to admit, but that's the only reason I took you to the school in the first place."

"Toyoko? Why her?" My pulse quickened. She hasn't done anything! I can vouch for that!"

He saw my anxiety and held his hand up again. "Now just a minute, Gil. Maybe you aren't in on this thing as much as I thought." He reflected a moment. "I thought you knew something when you nearly took my ears off in there after you saw that picture of her father."

"All I know is what some Jap girl told me---"

"Chieako?" he interrupted, and as he did I realized suddenly that here was my answer to the reason for Walt's visit to her apartment that night.

He was reading my mind again. "Oh, I knew what you were talking about that night in the barracks, Gil, when you were hinting that I had followed you. Hell, you should get an academy award for that!" He laughed briefly and continued, "You had every right to believe that something was fishy, and that's why I lied about being there. That way, if you had seen me you would start getting suspicious and maybe learn something."

"Suspicious!" I interrupted. "Hey, I even thought you were on the stuff for a while!"

"You know better now," he laughed, and then his face became serious again. "Now, this Hiashitani. I've been getting evidence on him, or at least trying to. That night at Chieako's apartment, I asked her several questions and she was somewhat helpful. The only thing I hadn't really planned on was running into you. But when I knew that you had seen me, I had to duck into my shell for a while, even though it's worked out all right now."

"Well, at least that explained why you forgot I existed," I said. "But what about Hiashitani?"

"Well, I have reason to believe that he could be the agent behind this heroin thing. Of course, he'd have quite a few accomplices. In fact, you know the administrator over at Nagaru---the one whose son was supposed to marry Toyoko?" I nodded. "Well, it seems that he takes quite a few trips over to Shanghai, and the most logical place for these drugs to come in from is China. Mind you," he pointed his cigarette at me, "I'm not certain of this yet. I'm still checking. That other man in the photo you just saw, by the way, was him."

"Well, I'll be damned! This thing goes a lot deeper than I expected!"

"You bet your life it's deep, and the thing we've got to be aware of is that no boners are pulled before we get the proof."

"Where do I fit into it now?"

"Well, I've thought all along that if you knew Toyoko better, you might be able to get something from the inside. Of course that's out now; she's been tossed---"

"She sure has, the son of a bitch!" I glowered. "And he's not even her own father..."

"What?" Walt grabbed me and I thought he was going to tear the front of my shirt. "What did you say?"

"I said he's not really her father...she told me."

"Are you sure?" He was pacing across the room now and I could nearly hear his mind working.

"They've never told her and they're not even aware that she knows it. Her parents adopted her when she was just a tyke...one of those mixed up messes. You see, her mother was Japanese and her father a Frenchman."

"How did she find out?" He stopped pacing and looked at me then.

"She checked her birth record in Tokyo while she was in college. Hell of a thing for her to find out."

"Hell of a thing, my eye! This could be what we're after. It could even be a motive..."

"A motive for what?" I interrupted. :"A guy doesn't need a motive to peddle dope!"

"Hey, think a minute, Gil! A man in his position would have to have a motive. He's got everything he needs in the way of position and money. But suppose somebody held something over his head...they could really raise hell with him!"

"Well, he's in a logical position for blackmail all right; damn near above suspicion, you might say. But what would the fact that Toyoko's not his daughter have to do with it?"

"I'm not sure just now." His fingers tapped restlessly on the wall as he leaned against it. "Let's just suppose that Toyoko is more than just a daughter. What if she were somebody special?"

I stood up and walked over to the print dryer. I looked, not really seeing it, as I said, "But that's all supposing; what if there's nothing to it? What then?"

"Well," he reflected, "It's something to shoot for, plus it could lead to something else, who knows? It may be way out in left field, but anything is better than nothing."

"What do we do?" I asked simply.

"The best thing for you to do is to go back with Toyoko and let on nothing is different."

"It's too late for that," I interrupted. "I flipped my lid this afternoon and told her I thought her father was mixed up in a dope racket."

"Hell! What did she say?"

"She took it hard…asked me if I had any proof. Fact is, I didn't have, so I apologized."

"Did you tell her where you heard it?"

"Yes, I told her about Chieako. Toy said she's known her a long time and that she didn't think Chieako would lie. That made me feel even worse."

"All we can hope for is that Toyoko doesn't do something rash, such as go to her father or…"

"Man!" I interrupted. "I really screwed it up!"

"Let's hope not," he concluded. "You'd better try to quiet her down. Get back there as quick as you can. In the meantime, I'm gonna try and catch a plane for Tokyo and have a look at some records myself."

He started for the darkroom then turned and stopped me again. "There's just one thing. If this gets around, we're sunk. These boys won't be playing if they discover that we're on their tail. So you keep a tight lip and be careful. Don't get creative on your own. And something else, I'm still Corporal Eckbart to you, nothing else."

I started to go out. "Aren't you coming?" I stopped.

"Just as soon as I dry these pictures, I'll be on my way too. And, by the way, that camera of yours is no damn good rusting away in your locker! It could come in handy." He smiled.

"Thanks," I said. "I'll take it along." I turned and walked away. The men were still playing poker in the corner when I reached the door and stepped out into the gathering darkness.

CHAPTER SEVENTEEN

I had taken the camera out of the locker and was unwrapping the film as Dale came over.

"Did you find Walt?"

I didn't look up as I slid the roll into the pocket. "Yea, I found him."

"I thought you would. He lives in that darkroom most of the time." He sat down on the bunk and watched. "The way you came in here with murder in your eyes, I thought…"

"Relax," I grinned. "He just welched on me, that's all. We were supposed to go down to Tokarazuka this weekend, only he got carried away with something else and forgot to meet me."

"Yea, he's a character all right," remarked Dale.

"Oh, he means well, but I'm afraid he's just forgetful." I snapped the case shut and reached for my jacket. As I did, the tiny ring box on the shelf caught my eye. I paused a moment, then took it down and shoved it into my pocket.

I started to go and he said, "Damn, don't you guys ever stay on base? Where're you off to now, Sarge?"

"To Tokarazuka; gonna take those pictures."

He jumped up. "I've never been there; mind if I come along?"

I laughed. "You're a little late, buddy. I just called a girl and she's going along. Let's take a rain check on it, though."

"A girl; I should have figured!" He grinned as he turned around. "O.K., some other time. I should stay here and save my okani anyway."

"Put it in munitions stocks," I said as I made my way around the bunk. "Scuttlebutt has it that we're in for a long war."

"Yup!" he grinned from his bunk, "Just think someday I'll have piles and piles, and piles…"

* * * *

We stood on the bridge for a time and watched. The river shown in the moonlight, and the tiny fishing boats far below seemed to glide along, ghost-like, hardly rippling the water as they moved slowly on their way. I looked up and the high mountains seemed to rise alongside like dark, strong shadows, as though they were huge protective beasts hiding the beauty and serenity of the valley from the cruelty of the outside world.

The strange beauty was overwhelming, as though one had suddenly stepped from a land of toil and strife into one of restfulness and peace.

I was glad she had suggested our getting away from the apartment, and it had only been a ten-minute train ride and a five-minute walk into this different world.

"I thought you would like it, Gil." She tossed her hair back as she turned to watch me. "I used to come to this spot many times when I was a little girl." She paused for a moment and looked up at the stars. "This was always my own…all this. When something went wrong with the rest of the world, somehow I could find peace here." She paused and looked my way. "I guess I'm acting like a little girl now. I'll stop."

"Not at all, Toy." I put my arm around her and held her close. "I can understand how you must have felt, for I feel that way now."

"Let's go down by the water." She tugged on my arm gently and we walked the short distance to the end of the bridge. There was a steep, winding path, and it was some time before we arrived breathless and laughing at the river's edge.

She sat down on the rocky shore to rest and I sat beside her, heaving a sigh as I relaxed.

We sat for some time, not speaking. Rather abruptly a group of fishing boats appeared from up-stream. They were filled with laughing and shouting people, and I watched with interest. Each boat was equipped with a large bright lantern which protruded far out over the bow, and they seemed to light up the river more, even though it was not yet dark outside.

"What's this all about?"

She had been watching intently and still didn't look my way. "They're Cormorant fishermen."

"What kind of a fish is that?" I asked.

"Oh, Cormorants aren't fish," she laughed. "They're birds…somewhat like a duck. They're trained to catch the fish."

"You mean they actually catch them and bring them to the boat?"

"No, pretty soon you will see what they do. They have the birds attached to long strings, and when a bird dives and catches a fish, the fisherman will pull him in and take the fish away."

"So the birds are really the fishermen!" I laughed.

"It's really quite a sport," she smiled. "They Cormorant fish every year about this time."

We watched for some time while many fish were brought in with much laughing, drinking and shouting. When they were nearly out of sight downstream, I turned and looked at Toyoko.

How lovely she looked in the moonlight; how beautiful was her silken hair, gently ruffling in the breeze. "I love you, Toyoko." I pulled her to me ever so gently and kissed her tenderly on the lips, and her eyes shown in the moonlight. I reached inside my pocket, took out the ring, then slowly lifted her hand and placed it on her finger.

"Oh, Gil! Gil!" she sobbed as she clung to me. "I'm so honored, and I love you so much…but I shouldn't…I really can't…"

Words no longer became necessary and all the love that had been held within a century of hearts seemed to be released at once. There on the pebbled bank of the river, two people were so desperately, perhaps hopelessly, in love.

It was nearly eleven o'clock when we took the train back to Garu, and as we neared the apartment I had the growing feeling that something was wrong – a feeling that everyone has sometimes, like a second sense that compelled me to stop near the doorway. Toyoko looked at me expectantly and said, "Why are we stopping? Let's go in."

I put my finger to my lips to quiet her, but it was too late. There was the resounding thumps of feet moving on the inside stairway, and I slid open the door quickly. The man paused at the foot of the steps and glanced our way for a split second, his face and features unrecognizable in the dim light. And then with a bound he ran down the hall. He hit the paper-matted shoji-screen and did not bother to slide it open, but smashed on through it.

I followed down the hall and paused long enough to slide what remained of the screen to one side. It had been all he needed, for when I ran into the backyard, there was nothing moving. I looked around hurriedly and then my eyes fell on the new house. It stood dark and quiet in the moonlight, and I ran to the doorway and stopped. Then cautiously I stepped up onto the little platform entrance where I edged my way forward enough to see into the room. Something moved quickly against the wall, and a whistling noise passed my head. I fell to the floor and as I did a form jumped to the window and was through it before I could recover. I shook as I pulled myself on to my feet again, and as I did my hand struck something. I looked up and a knife stuck out from the door jamb. The blood began to flow from a cut on my hand as I reached up and wrenched the knife free.

I was shaking as I left the step and started for the house. Toyoko met me with a rush.

"Gil! Gil, are you all right?" She reached me and I spun her back toward the doorway as I said, "Yea, I think so, but I almost wasn't! The son-of-a-bitch tossed a knife at me…nearly scored too!"

"Oh, Gil, I'm so scared," she shivered as we walked up the stairs.

"It could have been worse…I can't figure it out." I plunked into the chair and when she turned on the light she saw my hand.

She rushed over and grabbed me by the wrist. "You're hurt!" For a fleeting instant she looked pale as though she were about to faint, and then she quickly walked toward the cupboard. "I'll get something for you!" I watched her as she tore a pillow case into a long strip, and then she took a bottle from the shelf. I was lost in thought as she spread iodine over the cut and wrapped it. I took the knife from my pocket and slowly fingered it with the other hand. Walt had been right. They aren't playing around, and now they know for sure. I looked up at Toyoko. "After I told you about your father, did you talk to anybody about it?"

She paused and then, "I wasn't going to tell you, Gil, but I went over to see Chieako this afternoon, while you were gone."

"What happened?"

"We just talked…" She stopped wrapping then as tears welled into her eyes. "I had to, Gil; I had to know…and I wanted to hear it from her. After all, my father…"

"Did she tell you the same thing she told me?" I interrupted.

"Yes," she faltered, and it must be true, or at least something has to be wrong."

"Did you talk to anyone else about it? Your father, or…"

"No," she interrupted. "I couldn't do that. I thought of it, but somehow I couldn't."

"Girl, I'm glad you didn't!" I thought a moment as she finished wrapping my hand. Somehow they know I'm onto them. Hell, the only ones that know are Toy and Chieako, or Walt. Toy didn't say anything, and Walt certainly didn't either. I jumped up and grabbed my camera off the table.

"Gil! You aren't going out? Not now!" She reached for my arm and held me.

"Yes, Toy, but not for long."

She interrupted with a whimper, "I wasn't going to tell you this either, Gil…I'm afraid…"

"Of course you are, Toy! Hell, I'm scared too, especially after this." I motioned at my hand.

"No, you don't understand. I've been afraid for a long time now. I think someone has been following me ever since I stopped living at home, nearly three weeks now.

"Are you sure?" I grabbed her by the shoulders and stared at her.

"Yes…at first I thought I was just imagining things, but lately I've been almost certain. I saw a man, the same one, many times," she looked at the floor, wringing her hands. "Wherever I've gone, he's been there. I'm sure!"

"This explains why that joker was here tonight. If he saw you go to Chieako's place this afternoon, he knows that I'm on to something." I paused, reflecting, "But then, why did he run away? If he had been trying to kill me, he wouldn't have come here to do it and then run away; and why in hell was he following you in the first place, if it was him." Then Walt's words came back again. "What if she were something special, real special, and somebody found out?" I spun Toy around toward me again.

"Listen, Honey, you close those doors and windows, and don't let anyone else in. I don't care who it is. No one!"

"Please, Gil. Don't go out now. Wait until tomorrow." She tried to hold me back and I pulled her to me and kissed her gently.

"No just be calm. I won't be gone long." I threw the camera over my shoulder and left her standing in the center of the room.

CHAPTER EIGHTEEN

The light was on in the window of Chieako's apartment. I paused as the thought of going up there again stopped me cold. The combination of the Fall wind and the situation forced me to shiver and I stood there in the dark for several minutes, wondering if I had the guts to go through with it. I tried to think, but my mind drew a blank, so I went in and carefully moved up the stairway until I stood on the landing beside the door.

The sound of voices talking in Japanese came through, but I couldn't understand a single word. Chieako was speaking; I knew her voice by now, but the other was deep and one I had never heard: A man's voice. It was all in low monotone. Now and then came the clink of china. I waited for several minutes, then took the knife out of my belt and reached out, sliding the screen open quickly.

Chieako was so surprised that she just stared, but the squat little Jap in the gray overcoat dropped his cup and nearly choked on his tea.

No one spoke as I started toward him with the knife exposed. Then suddenly the table came up and hit me squarely across the gut. The guy was on top of me, breathing down my neck before I could recover. His grip on my arm was too strong to break and the knife slipped away and I found myself sailing through space. Judo! I regained my feet and blinked to focus my eyes again. This time he hadn't run and apparently had no intentions of doing so. The knife glistened in his hand now and he approached me quickly. I can still see that deadly smile as he advanced and then at the last instant I brought my foot up, catching him square in the groin. He reeled backward and fell across the doorway, gasping for breath, one hand still grasping the knife and the other clutching his waist. I started for him again as he turned and with all the strength he had left, he tried to crawl toward the stairs. I reached him as he arrived at the top step and again my foot found its mark. He pitched forward screaming and tumbled head long down the stairs, coming to rest at the bottom in a crumpled heap. He wasn't moving, so I staggered back to the door. I looked around frantically for a moment but it was evident that Chieako had left during the scuffle. I picked my camera up off the floor and examined it to see if it was broken, then started to throw it over my shoulder. I stopped and opened it up, set the speed and slid the flashgun and bulb into place. He was lying face down and I turned him over with my foot. As I did, his head flopped crazily to one side and I saw that his neck was broken. The thought that he was dead turned my blood cold. I began to shake again, but finally lifted the camera and snapped the shutter.

I walked out slowly and no one was around. Then my steps became quicker and I didn't stop until I arrived out of breath in front of the house.

I ran up the steps and knocked softly on the screen. There was a shuffle inside and Toyoko cried, "Who is it?"

"Gil! Open up!"

Cautiously I slide the screen aside and stepped in, not seeing her at first. When I did, Chieako ducked behind Toy and threw her hand up.

I reached Toyoko and pulled her to one side. As I started for the girl, she cowered backward against the wall, and I was almost upon her when Toy grabbed me by the arm.

"No, Gil! No!" she screamed, "Wait a minute. I can explain!"

I looked at her, not really seeing her in my mad frenzy, and retorted, "What do you mean, NO! This little bitch deserves it...I found her talking with that guy who damn near killed me. What the hell is this anyway; she's as two-faced as...!"

"You don't understand," she interrupted, stepping between us. "Chieako didn't know he was ever involved in anything bad."

"Well, you can tell her for me that the little bastard's dead as a door knob. I broke his damn neck!"

There was a sob and then a sigh as Chieako fell to the floor with a thud. She had fainted and Toy ran to her side. With a cry she looked up at me then, and I had to sit down after she had spoken. "Gil, he was her brother!"

I shook violently as I sat there and tried to light a cigarette. "No! My God, I've killed the wrong man! What in hell have I done anyway!"

Toy had run to the kitchen, and she spoke again as she bent over Chieako now, holding a wet towel on her forehead. "She knows now, Gil; I told her about the man who had been following me, and she showed me this picture of her brother." She took it from her pocket and extended it toward me. I grabbed it quickly and it was him. "He was the man who followed me, and the same one who was here in our apartment tonight, but she never knew this, and now, well she just couldn't take it!"

I sat down again and threw my hand up to my forehead. So I hadn't gotten the wrong man after all! Thank God!

"He must have gone over to her place after he slipped out of here," I said dumbly. "What was I supposed to think when I found him there? Naturally, I thought that she…"

"I'm afraid she didn't know, Gil." Her voice was calmer now and she attended to Chieako affectionately. "All this, well, I think I'd have passed out too."

"Let's put her in the bedroom," I said as I got up. "It's a lot more comfortable there." I picked Chieako up, carried her into the bedroom, and laid her down gently on the bed. Toy stayed there and I wandered aimlessly back to the living room where I stared absently out of the window for a long time. I was tired and my side ached relentlessly. I didn't even notice Toyoko until she had closed the screen and walked up behind me.

"She's sleeping now," she said quietly as she put her arm around me.

I turned then. "My God, Toy, how could I know? All I knew was that somebody had tried to kill me. He'd have done it too if I hadn't been lucky. But her brother…that's a little sickening." I paused a moment. What I can't understand is how come she didn't know, with all this going on under her nose."

"She's had a feeling that something was wrong for a long time now, Gil, but she really didn't know what it was. Not until you busted in there tonight. That's why she came here. She told me about it and nearly collapsed when I told her it had been her brother who was following me around. But when you said he was dead, well, that really did it."

"What I'm wondering is what do I do now," I reflected. "My life, in fact the lives of all three of us, won't be worth a dime when this gets out." My thoughts returned to her father and I asked, "Did you ever see that man around your house or ever talking with your father?"

She thought a moment and then answered a little hesitantly, "No, I don't think so... In fact, I never saw him before until he began following me around...Chieako said that he was working in Negaru until recently, and that he had suddenly dropped in on her a few weeks ago."

"Negaru," I repeated more to myself than to her. "The other guy in Walt's picture, he was the Administrator of Negaru." I wonder...but there are probably half a million people in this town from Negaru, so it might not mean a thing. And yet, if it did, it might be worth something. There was just one more thing. I turned to Toyoko.

"Toy, you told me that your father had been a French Ambassador. Was there anything else that you saw on the records – anything special?" I looked at her carefully.

"No, although I don't know what you mean by 'something special'. I know what his name was, though."

"What is it?" I asked anxiously.

"Maurice. Maurice Duprey," she said absently. "I even looked him up in the records at the Embassy, but I decided that a man who would do such a thing wasn't much of a father, or that perhaps he didn't even know about me." Her voice dropped off and she walked over to the chair and sat down.

"Well, suppose he knows about you now and should want you back?"

"I doubt if I'd be interested," she said matter-of-factly.

I had an idea and I walked back over to her. "Toy, I'm going out again, but not for long."

"Why?" She straightened up.

"I'm going to make a phone call. I'll go down to the club; it won't take long."

She started to get up and for a moment I thought she was going to protest again, but instead she sat back down. "If you have to, but please don't be gone long."

"I'll be back in a jiffy," I said, and bent down and kissed her. "Close the place up again and this time do as I say – don't let anyone in."

As I neared the Club First Chance, the commotion up the street caught my eye. A crowd had gathered and as I continued to walk on, an ambulance came blaring up the street and screeched to a halt in front of Chieako's apartment.

I entered the Club and headed for the phone booth. It was behind the dance floor, an alcove with no door, and I thought for a moment the noise of the crowd and the juke box might make it impossible to make the call.

I hesitated, then plugged one ear with a finger and picked up the phone clumsily with my bandaged hand. I gave the operator the number of the base and there was a few minutes while she flustered to herself interpreting it. Finally there was a buzz and the base operator answered, "Camp Garu. Number please."

"Give me C-Barracks, Headquarters Company," I said, and waited. There were a few more minutes of buzzing before a sleepy voice answered.

"Yes?"

"Who is this?"

"Corporal Harding. Who in hell is this?"

"Sgt. Gilman," now...

"Come on Sarge, at this time of night...."

"I'm well aware of the time, Corporal." I interrupted angrily. "Is Dale there in the barracks?"

"Yea, I think so – just a minute and I'll check."

There was a thump as he dropped the phone onto the desk and I waited impatiently. Finally dale picked up the phone and asked sleepily, "Hello, Admiral, what in hell you want this time of night?"

"Dale, listen...I want you to do me a favor..."

"A favor? Good God, now? Look Sarge, I'm standing here in my shorts, freezing my ass off at one o'clock in the morning and you want me...!"

"Look, this is important!" I yelled. The noise in the background was deafening and I felt that I had to shout to make myself heard. "I want you to go to the office and look up a man for me in the files."

"Oh, hell, Sarge! You're drunk! Now why in hell don't you go on and have your fun and I'll go back to bed!"

"Listen, I'm not drunk, and if you don't do this, I'm gonna play lawnmower with your ass, cold or not!"

"I still think you're drunk, but I'll do it.! His voice became a little more rational and then, "Now who is this mystery man you want me to look up?"

"Good," I said. "He's a Frenchman, Maurice Duprey..."

"What was it?"

"Duprey! Maurice Duprey!" I almost shouted.

There was a moment of silence and then a laugh. "Hell, I don't have to look him up; he's no mystery...even I know who he is."

"You do?"

"Yea. You forget apparently that I'm a miser myself, so why shouldn't I know another one?

"Well, who is he?"

:He used to be in the French Government, big wheel of some sort, I'm not sure just what he was then, but I know who he is now."

"Who?" I nearly screamed at him.

"Just about the richest French kisser on the Island of Sumatra, that's all. I read an article on him about a month ago."

"What else?" I interrupted.

"Well, he's got rubber trees growing out of both of his pretty little latex ears, and he keeps house in Singapore. In Malaya."

"Dale, you're a real jewel! That's just what I wanted."

"And did you know that most of the rain falls on Sumatra in the afternoon, which leaves the mornings clear for gathering the latex...and that rubber trees are brittle and damaged easily by strong winds, which explains why Sumatra is best.."

"O.K. funny man, so you're smart!"

"Yes, but now I'm afraid you know my secret!" he laughed.

"What secret?"

"Those guys back in school used to call me the Walking Encyclopedia. I'd appreciate it if it didn't get around...you know, me being a lowly Private and all."

"I'll see that the whole world finds out!" I retorted. "I'm afraid you've strained your brain enough for tonight, so I'll let you get your rest. So long."

He started to say, "What's this all..." But I dismissed it as I dropped the phone back on the hook.

CHAPTER NINETEEN

When I left the Club First Chance the street outside was deserted. I hurried on with impatient steps and the pain in my side and hand faded away as I walked.

The whole thing was taking shape now, and so far Walt's idea fell in to the very letter...Toy must be someone special. But one thought struck that just didn't seem to jive with the rest---why would Toyoko's father toss her out if he had been forced to go along with the racket because of her? It didn't seem right that he would let her so much as out of his sight, even though there had been this marriage bit. The guy had been this Negaru Administrator's son...that could fit in somewhere.

My mind stopped working as I knocked softly on the door. Toy slid it open far enough to see, and I remember there was an anxious and frightened look on her face as I stepped in. Then the look faded away into blackness as I felt myself falling...

"Gil! Gil! Wake up!"

My whole body ached and I must have cried out as I tried to sit up and fell back. The hand and side felt as though knives were piercing them slowly, and my head refused to hold still as my eyes tried to stop the room from moving.

Someone was bending over me and I could hear the slaps on my face, but I could not feel them for several moments. "Gil! For God's sake! Come on..."

The words rang in my ears like bells, and then slowly the waving face in front of me took form. Walt! I tried again, and this time I got up on my elbows, where I hovered while trying to shake the constant buzz from my ears.

"What happened?" His anxious and worried face stared at me a little clearer now, and I gradually regained control. When I did, I nearly yelled.

"Where's Toy, and Chieako?"

"There's no one else here, just you and me." Walt stopped me gently as I tried to get up.

"They were right here, just a while ago!"

"When? This morning ?"

"Morning?" I shouted and this time I made it to my feet, where I leaned breathlessly against the wall. "Hell, what time is it anyway?"

"Almost ten o'clock…"

"Christ! Don't tell me I've been out all this time. Where's Toy?" I repeated it again as my heart pounded violently.

"She's not here now, Gil…neither is Chieako. When were they here?"

I gathered my wits about me slowly as I tried to recall and relate to him in detail the events that had occurred during the night. When I reached the part about the phone call to Dale, he stopped puffing on his cigarette and jumped out of his chair.

"Is he sure?"

"Yeah, I've discovered that Dale's a pretty reliable source," I answered, "and besides, it figures, doesn't it?"

"Does it ever!" He slapped his hands together as he paced around the little room, and I watched him expectantly. "This all fits in with what I found out in Tokyo…" he paused and looked at me quickly. "You sure you killed that guy?"

"Positive." I answered numbly.

"Then we've really got to be careful, and particularly you! Hell man, you're nothing but a duck in a shooting gallery now! Can you walk?"

"Yeah, I think so, but what about Toy and Chieako? We've got to find them!"

"That's just what we're going to do, if it's not too late! Come on, I'll explain it to you. We can grab a cab outside."

My limbs and body had grown stiff during sleep, but as he helped me down the stairs and I walked out into the street the circulation began to move again, and by the time we had reached the corner I could move freely. The pain was there yet but the thought of getting to Toyoko pushed it back into secondary importance.

I waited for Walt to start explaining and when he didn't, I looked at him impatiently. "Well?"

"Well what?"

"Well, what gives?"

"Just hold on a minute; we'll get a cab."

One came up the street as he said it, and I whistled. The guy pulled over and we climbed into the tiny back seat. When Walt told the driver to take us to Camp Garu, I nearly lost my head. "Back to Camp! I thought we…"

"Look, you want to find Toy, don't you?" He looked at me calmly.

"Hell yes, but she's not at the base!"

"No, I know that, but you and I would stand about as much chance of finding her alone as we would fighting the entire Marine Corps. We're going to the base and get some help."

"The C.I.D.! Why? Can't we call them from here? Anyway, I'll bet a million she's at her old man's house!"

"I wouldn't take that bet," he retorted slowly, "but if she is, we'd still need help, and I'm not risking this whole damn thing by making a phone call!"

I realized that he was right and calmed down as we bounced along the road.

"Man, I wish you hadn't killed that guy. That's gonna be hard to explain."

"Explain," I interrupted, "that shouldn't be hard. It was self-defense!" I paused a moment and then said, "Besides I got his picture." I stopped and reached frantically for the camera. It was gone!. "Did you see my camera back there anywhere?"

"No," Walt answered. "Whoever it was that zapped you probably took it. You'll get it back. Besides, a picture of a dead man wouldn't help."

"Wow," I breathed. "I must be a jinx! First I nearly get knifed, then I kill a guy besides getting slugged over the crown and losing Toy. Now I've even lost my Argus."

"Relax," he laughed. "It could have been worse!"

"Yeah, I could be dead. Next time I might not be so lucky."

"You're right," he paused a moment. "In fact, you know the only reason I got you into this mess was for information. It's gone a lot farther than that now. You're in pretty bad shape anyway, and from here on it's a matter for the police. Maybe you should stay at the base, go to the infirmary and get yourself fixed up."

"You're kidding!" I yelled at him. "If you think for one minute you can get me into something like this and then tell me hands off, you're---"

"O.K.! O.K.!" He grinned as he held up a hand. "I knew it all along...just checking. But you know what we're in for."

"No, I don't, to be honest about it. But I do know that I love Toy and getting her out of this mess is what I want. Hell of a lot of good I'd be sitting on my ass in the infirmary chewing on aspirin tablets!"

"Look Gil, we're almost there, and I've got to explain this whole damn mess to Major Vette. Wait, and you'll hear it all then."

I started to protest but the main gate suddenly loomed up in front of us and instead I reached into my pocket for the I.D. card.

CHAPTER TWENTY

The Corporal at the desk looked up with a sneer when Walt asked for Major Vette.

"The Major? On Sunday afternoon? You nuts? He's sacked out. I wish this base had a golf course, then at least we'd know where to find him on a weekend."

I thought Walt was going to bound right over the desk and tear him apart, but instead he leaned over and looked the little guy square in the face.

"Look, Corporal! I'm not nuts, and if you don't get the Major on that phone right now, I'm going to put you on report!" His eyes burned into the kid and he suddenly jumped up.

"Oh, excuse me Sir, I thought…"

"I don't give a damn what you thought! Now get the Major on that line!"

"Yes, Sir," he said meekly as he gulped. Within a minute he had him on and he handed the phone over to Walt. "The Major, sir."

Walt sat down on the edge of the desk; then he motioned the Corporal out of the room before he spoke. "Hello, Major Vette? This is Lieutenant Eckbart." There was a long pause and then, "I know you don't know any Lieutenant Eckbart, and I'm well aware that it's Sunday afternoon, but this is of utmost importance…yes, it is. Can you come over to your office right away? Yes, sir, I'll explain when you get here… No, I can't tell you over the phone…yes, sir."

We waited for the Major and he arrived in less than five minutes. It was definite that he had been caught napping as he still sported an old sweat shirt and wrinkled khaki trousers and his graying hair was disheveled. He was a tall, athletic-looking individual and walked in with his steel gray eyes flicking back and forth.

"Well, which one of you is Eckbart?" he finally asked.

"I am, sir." Walt was reaching into his hip pocket with one hand as he motioned to me with the other. "This is Sergeant Gillaney."

"Glad to know you, sir," I started to say, but he didn't pay me any attention. He turned his attention to Walt.

"Here, this might help." Walt handed a small folder to the Major and he looked at it closely for a minute. Finally, he glanced up, but cautiously.

"Well, I'll be damned! Why wasn't I informed that you were here? How long you been on base?"

"About three months, sir," Walt answered as he took back his I.D. card. "I've been working on this dope business."

"So that's it," the Major stomped over and put one foot up on a chair. "I might have known they'd pull something like this on me. Damn, what am I supposed to be anyway, incompetent?"

"It's not that, sir," Walt hurried a reply. "Headquarters thought that you were known too well to get in on this thing from the inside. I was given leads and sent over here to do that part."

"Leads! What kind of leads? They could have given them to me."

"That wouldn't have helped, Major. Again, you're known too well."

Walt was making sense and the Major knew it, so he suddenly calmed down and spoke in a milder tone.

"O.K., I get it. So now, what have you got?" He lit up a cigarette and studied Walt as though expecting to hear some fantastic story he could sneer at.

"First of all, you asked about leads," Walt snuffed a cigarette into an ashtray and shoved his hands into his pockets, looking at the Major. "One of them was of the possibility of a newly organized 'Soshi' gang."

The Major had a rather blank look, so Walt continued. "I'll refresh your memory on it. The original rulers of Japan, hundreds of years ago, were known as Daimio. These rulers hired bodyguards, fighting men, the ones commonly known as 'Samurai.' When the Daimio were overthrown by a central government, a good many of these Samurai, then out of jobs, banded together in groups. They were very organized and became known as Soshi. They were more of a band of thugs and professional assassins than anything else, and most of them became attached to various politicians. They were open in everything they did then, and rented themselves out by the hour, day or even a year, exchanging their services for so little as food and clothing. To make it short, they did the dirty work for their employer, like ruining a competitor's business or even murdering arrival politicians." He paused a moment and I sat there wondering what he was leading up to.

"There were, of course, certain stipulations in the agreement," he continued. "In case a Soshi was arrested his employer was expected to pay him handsomely for his time in prison, and occasionally to even send him a few luxuries during his prison term. Well, in spite of all these under-handed dealings, the Soshi have always considered themselves intensely patriotic toward their country, and they have always been active in stirring up Anti-American forms of agitation. Needless to say, during World War Two these men were in great demand by the Japanese as fighting men."

"I appreciate all this background, but what does it have to do with all this?" The Major interrupted as he leaned heavily on the desk and looked at Walt questioningly.

"Well, over a year ago a similar type of dope ring was operating near Tachekawa Air Base in Tokyo. Some of them were finally caught and imprisoned, but not all. What really matters is that the Soshi were indicated in it, as several of its members had formerly been associated with Soshi bands. The one thing that makes it difficult is that they've reorganized since the old days. They're not the run of the mill thugs they once were; in fact, some of those located in the Tokyo area were prominent businessmen. There were even some college students." Walt looked over at me then added, "Even school teachers."

I started to speak but Major Vette beat me to it. "So that brings us to what?"

"To Garu." Walt stated flatly as he walked around the edge of the desk. "I've checked records on Hiashitani, the Mayor of the city." The Major nodded that he was aware of this fact, "and about twenty years ago when Hiashitani was pulling for office, he was associated with one of the Soshi groups."

"What are you driving at?" The Major raised his eyebrows and it was evident by his confused expression that he was still trying to grasp things.

Walt raised a hand and chuckled slightly. "O.K., O.K., I only wanted to answer your first question about the leads. Now I think I'd better go back to the beginning of the recent mess we've been stumbling into."

With that he started right from scratch, and as he related the discoveries, the Major cast an eye at me.

"Hell, Sergeant, you look as though you should be in the hospital!" As he spoke I could imagine myself, hair askew on my head, two days' growth of beard, clothes torn and wrinkled, my arm bandaged up, and an overall lack of sleep that all together probably made me look like the living dead. I damn near nodded agreement with him, but I checked it and faked a look of capability as he turned back to Walt.

"That brings me around to those trips to Tokyo," Walt continued. "We've thought for some time there was a connection between Hiashitani and his adopted daughter's father, Maurice Duprey. Now this Duprey is a former French Ambassador who at present has himself quite a rubber business in Sumatra." He paused a moment in thought before continuing, "which is where another fellow enters the picture: That's Yoshu Hiamatsu, the present Administrator of the city Nagaru. Now, there is a connection between these three that isn't at all natural. First of all, Hiamatsu and Hiashitani are old friends, but it goes deeper. When adoption papers were drawn up, Hiamatsu was the legal witness present, and he signed the papers as such. Now that would seem natural enough, except that the records also show that he at the time was an employer of Duprey's at the embassy." Major Vette picked up a little and watched Walt carefully now. "Another of my leads was that Hiamatsa had been taking a lot of flights from Tokyo to Shanghai lately, so I checked this out at Japan Air Lines' main office. It's true, and the other thing that's amazing about it is that on these dates, Maurice Duprey takes regular flights from Singapore to Shanghai. He's cagey at it too. Instead of taking the regular route through Manilla, he goes to Chungking, and then to Shanghai. I had a helluva time getting that info, but some yen and about two more hours of ear-bending on the phone finally did it."

I whistled out in amazement, and the Major stood up and paced around the desk. When he had made the tour several times, he stopped in front of Walt again.

"If all this is correct, then Duprey could be using Hiamatsu as a go between, and trying to get his daughter back---"

"We thought of that," Walt interrupted. "But about a month ago a deal was set between the two administrators – a deal for Hiamatsu's son and Hiashitani's daughter to get married. The girl, Toyoko, refused and the old boy tossed her out on her ear. But it could be that if Hiashitani was being threatened, he would do it to help his daughter, not so much to be mean."

Walt interrupted him abruptly as he stood up. "And Hiamatsu had to go along with it, or he'd get caught in the middle. Now, if Duprey had wanted his daughter back bad enough, he could have forced Hiashitani into the dope racket, set him up as a distributor, under a threat, and," he paused a moment, "that would indicate that the whole adoption wasn't according to Hoyle."

You mean that Toy's old man isn't really the rotten bastard we've figured?" I had been listening in silence and suddenly came to life.

"That depends on how you look at it." Walt glanced my way with a wrinkled forehead. "As far as Toy's concerned, he may have meant the best by throwing her out, but even so I can't see where he's the better. Anybody who pushed that stuff to servicemen isn't a good egg!"

"But if he were forced into it…"

"If the adoption wasn't legal, then it's almost certain he was forced, and had to go along to keep the girl."

"Now we're getting somewhere!" Vette had the expression of a cat about to pounce on a one-winged pigeon. "I'll get word through immediately to intelligence in Singapore and we'll get the low-down on this Duprey. There's only one thing." The expression vanished as he continued, "Hiashitani certainly isn't passing this stuff on by himself, and we've got to get the whole works or nothing at all. That's not going to be easy!"

"I've got one more thing." Walt rubbed his whiskers. "I've got a picture of the two of them, Hiamatsu and Hiashitani. This particular one I snapped exactly one week ago, last Sunday evening to be exact." He took out a smaller copy of the one I had seen and handed it to Vette. "I've seen the two of them together three times now, and each time it was the same – Sunday evening around seven o'clock. That's one of the reasons we're here now. We've got a few hours to go yet and we could possibly catch them during a transaction. As far as how the stuff gets from there to the men, that's another thing…" His voice trailed off and it was apparent that he was waiting for something from the Major.

I interrupted instead. "What about Toy and Chieako? For Heaven's sake, those guys know something's taking place and they're liable to have done away with them by now." I paused, then, "or they might even be waiting for us!"

"You're right about that," the Major looked at me with concentration. "We can't go off half-cocked." He rubbed his stubbled chin for a moment. "You've killed one of them, you're certain of that?"

"Positive," I said. "His neck was broken. He was Chieako's brother."

He was pacing around again and neither Walt nor I interrupted his thought. Finally he stopped and hammered his fist down on the desk. "O.K.! We can't wait for any more info; we've got to act right now if we want to catch them at all! Now here's what you guys do. While I get word to Intelligence and the Military Police, I want you to go back to Hiashitani's place…"

We were hardly breathing as we listened and occasionally glanced back and forth in wonder, and thinking back, with fear as well.

CHAPTER TWENTY-ONE

"You got the whole thing straight now?" Walt nudged me.

"Yeah," I barely whispered, as I realized for the first time that my knees were shaking. Then I patted the forty-five that was nestled in the shoulder holster, trying hard to draw comfort from it. It was cold and offered no relief.

Walt reached forward to touch the driver on the shoulder, said something in Japanese, and the cab came to a halt on the narrow street. We stepped out and watched the tiny vehicle go out of sight.

"Why're we getting out here? It's several more blocks to the place." I looked at him and realized how odd he seemed standing there in the kimono and the geta shoes. The girl in C.I.D. had asserted herself and had done a good job. His eyes were even pulled out slightly and she had somehow given his skin, hands and face a golden tan.

"I wouldn't mind getting out in front of their house myself, but you'd get cut down quicker than hell in those civvies. We'll go according to plan. I'll go ahead now and you wait about two minutes before coming in the other way. Got it?"

"Yeah, I've got it." My knees were still knocking and it must have been conspicuous.

"Look, Gil, if everything comes off all right, we've nothing to fear. Now, it's nearly seven so I'll get going. Watch yourself and be careful." He turned and the wooden shoes clopped loudly as he walked down the street, turned at the corner and disappeared.

I pulled the jacket a little tighter around my neck and leaned back against the high fence. I wanted a cigarette then, but shook off the feeling. Several people passed by with hardly a glance my way but my nerves made me look at each one as though expecting to see an enemy. Two minutes were nearly up when a car screeched around the corner and its headlights swung squarely on me as it turned. I lowered my head and shoved my hands into the jacket pockets as it drove on by and squealed into another street.

I walked on down and around the corner. The house sat nearly a block up the street and I looked frantically for the back alley Walt had said was there. I had passed several homes and was thinking that I had missed it when I saw the path – a narrow strip not more than three feet wide, bordered on both sides by high boundary fences. I glanced both ways, then stepped in and walked slowly toward the end of the walls. The silence was eerie, and not even a breath of air moved. Finally, from behind one of the walls came muffled laughter and talking, and even though I was on the outside, the sound seemed to calm my nerves.

At the end of the path was a small plot of unused ground, very scarce in this over-populated city, and along one side was another of those high, vine-covered fences. I turned left and followed that one to the end of the plot.

This one at the end would be Hiashitani's. I stepped cautiously for the last few paces and when a wall finally confronted me, I searched frantically for an opening or a knot hole to peer through into the yard. It was air-tight and looked to be about nine feet high. There was not even a cross member to crawl up on. I stood in confusion for several moments, not knowing which way to turn. If I made a running jump, someone could possibly hear it. That was out, but what other alternative did I have? I finally got down on my knees and started crawling along, feeling the boards as I went, and when one felt loose, I would try a slight tug at the bottom. I had gone nearly fifty feet and was nearing the end of the fence when a board gave as I pulled. I noticed as I pulled again that not only one board, but four in a row swung out heavily, and I breathed a sigh of relief when a harder pull revealed a hinged section which swung upward. It was a hole about three feet high and around three feet across, and I heaved the door upward far enough to see inside. My joy was short-lived as inside was nothing but blackness.

The thought that I wasn't entering the yard at all suddenly occurred to me, as there was no light from a house or any other illumination, but it was too late and there was no other entrance.

I lifted the gate upward and crawled through. The feeling of dampness was everywhere and as I felt around I discovered that I was in what seemed to be a cement tunnel about three feet square. I took my lighter out cautiously and flicked it.

The little light hardly wavered in the unmoving musty air, and its illumination showed nothing but blackness ahead. I put the lighter away and crawled along, conscious of the blood pounding in my head as I moved. I crawled carefully for what may have been about twenty yards, and was ready to halt and rest when my hand fell onto something soft. Cloth! I groped further and a shudder shook my entire body as my hand grasped a cold arm. I drew back quickly and fumbled for the lighter again. I was ready to light it when footsteps sounded directly over my head. They passed by and my hand shook violently as I lit the lighter. Toyoko! My heart nearly stopped! No! It was Chieako! She lay there ghost-like, unmoving, and her white face and open eyes seemed to be staring through me.

The footsteps were coming back, and I looked upward in haste. Women's heels! Or perhaps, geta shoes! But suppose it was a woman, maybe Toyoko? The steps stopped directly over my head and I noticed that the ceiling was wood now, not cement. I closed the cover on the lighter carefully and didn't move. The steps finally moved on again, and I lifted myself cautiously over the body of Chieako. I began crawling again, only this time I had not gone ten feet when my head hit cement. It was the end of the tunnel, and I looked up again. This time a faint ray of light ran along the edge of a board overhead. I leaned back on my knees and reached up, running my finger along the crevice. Where the light stopped, so did the board, and again I lit the lighter. A framed trap door outlined itself, and as I looked my mind ran wild.

This is all too easy! My God, I'm right under his house, probably the living room! I glanced frantically at the illuminated dial on the watch – ten minutes after seven. If everything went off all right, Walt should be in there by now! The idea had been for him to join the rest of the pushers when they arrived, and to enter the house…if they arrived! We knew there was a possibility that the exchange would be called off, and even a chance that someone would be lying in wait.

The one thing that we were hoping for was that Hiashitani wouldn't fly the coop before we arrived, but now that we were on to him, the only thing he would be successful at would be a quick finish for us! Therefore, a trap seemed to be the obvious thing to expect, and Walt had probably stumbled into it, make-up and all! That fear became more and more over-powering as the silence continued overhead, and my hand went to the forty-five again. This time I lifted it from the holster and palmed it nervously.

The voice of a woman came piercingly through – she was humming nervously in low Japanese syllables, quickly and quietly. Toyoko! I crumbled as I thought of her, probably locked in the room overhead. If this was so, she would probably be alone. I started to reach up to lift the trap door when I heard the sirens…they were faint at first, but as I listened, they grew louder. Finally they stopped completely. Then, as the sound of shots rang out, I threw the door back. The light hit me with a blinding glare and I looked up into the face of Toyoko. She had stepped directly in front of me, and her hand flew to her mouth in complete surprise. "Gil!!"

I lifted myself from the tunnel as she backed away. "Toy! Are you okay?" I stepped to her quickly and grabbed her.

"Gil!. Oh Gil! How…how?" Her voice fluttered as I drew backward.

"I'll explain later, Toy! Where's your father? I heard shots!" I nearly shouted as I thought of Walt.

"In the house – that way…! She pointed waveringly with her hand to a door at the end of the room.

The sound of more shots rang out and I ran to the door. Instead of the usual screen, the door was solid wood, and I pulled on the handle in vain.

"It's locked." She watched me carefully as I turned around, and I noticed that there was no trace of tears or hysteria, and her voice was suddenly very calm. She walked over to a desk near the side of the room as she talked. "I've been locked in here since last night, Gil. There's no way out; I've tried."

"This isn't part of the house at all?" I asked nervously.

"No, this is the kura, a separate building where my father keeps his valuables…"

Her voice trailed off, and as it did the shouting and the noise of the shooting suddenly stopped. I grew more anxious.

"I'll yell…they'll hear us!" I yelled several times in the direction of the door, and when I turned around again she was standing beside the trap in the floor. She had turned sideways from me and one hand was completely out of my sight.

105

I noticed with a start that her eyes were suddenly hard and her face drawn, not at all like the Toyoko I had grown to love, and as the thought struck me, so did something else that pained even deeper. With every ounce of effort and breath in me, I asked the one question I hoped would clear my doubts.

"You…you've been locked in here alone?"

"Yes, since last night." Her voice stopped suddenly as she looked at me squarely and lifted her chin.

"Then how did Chieako…" I was stopped short as she turned completely around and faced me. The pistol in her hand did not waver as she directed it at my mid-section!

My own gun was pointing at her as it must have been ever since I had asked her that question. I tightened unconsciously on the grip.

"That is something I can't wait to explain now…But Toy….I've loved you," I cried out. "My God! I still do!" I started toward her blindly.

The bark of her little pistol rang out and I was thrown violently backward. My left arm swung crazily, but there was no feeling in it as I sagged to my knees.

She was lowering herself into the hole and my eyes picked out the foggy shape of her head and shoulder still above the floor.

My arm jumped high in the air and the little cement building seemed to rock on its foundations as the roar of my forty-five filled the kura. Toyoko's blurred figure disappeared through the opening with a resounding thud, and with it a shattered and torn dream…I felt all the pain and sickness of one who no longer cared to live. Unable to see any longer, I retched violently several times as I fell forward into the welcome blackness.

CHAPTER TWENTY-TWO

"**W**ell, you've finally decided to join the rest of the working class!"

The words seemed to be coming through from the 500-yard line, and I fought to bring them within range. As my eyes finally opened and closed, the light blue sky overhead gradually changed to an aqua ceiling, and there was no pain as I turned my head. Walt sat there grinning. "Where the...?"

"Take it easy a minute and try to get your bearings again," he cautioned as he motioned with his hand.

"Seems...seems like I've gone through all this before..." I faltered slowly.

He lit a cigarette and stuffed it in the corner of his mouth, smiling out the other side. "I'd give you one if I thought you could handle it. It'd probably help keep your mouth shut, but those pretty nurses around here would frown on the idea." He got up and put one foot on a chair, leaning over the edge of the bed. "You know something? Every time I find you, you're out on your feet like this. 'Fraid you set a new record for yourself this time though – three days!"

"Three days!" I would have sat up but as I tried a pain shot through my left side that made me gasp for breath.

"That's right, three days. You're okay though. They've had you full of dope...you took quite a nasty rap on the shoulder." He stopped quickly as though changing his mind about something and continued with, "You'll be good as new with a couple of weeks' rest."

My mind was still too foggy to think, and it took a few minutes for his words to sink in. When they did, I started to speak, but he interrupted me as he suddenly straightened up.

"Hey, what the hell am I doing, anyway? I'd better tell the Doc you're back with us!" He started quickly toward the door. "I'll come back later, Gil, and we'll talk the whole thing over."

I broke into a sweat as events were suddenly flying back into my mind. I started to cry out after him, but the door was swinging back and forth and he had gone. I watched the movement of the door, and it hadn't come to a complete stop before it opened wide again and a man in white walked in. He smiled broadly as he approached the bed.

"Glad to see you've come around, son. I'll have to admit that you gave us some wild betting at first, but it looks like you're going to be okay now." I watched him as he adjusted his stethoscope and came slowly toward me. "How one man could wind up in the condition you did and still live, is amazing!"

That was all it took, and his voice and face slipped slowly out of sight as I passed out again.

Two days later I was sitting up leaning on a pillow when Walt sauntered in. He was wearing a uniform with little gold bars gleaming from the shoulders. I ignored them completely as I yelled, "Well, where in hell you been?"

He threw up both hands in a friendly gesture. "Careful buddy, you'll have a relapse!" My eagle then pulled a chair alongside the bed and perched himself over the back of it. "I suppose you've been doing lots of brainwork..."

"Brainwork! Hell, what else can a man do in a joint like this? I'm punched like a dartboard, scrubbed raw twice a day, and in general told to keep calm! Now how in hell can a man take it easy with all that going on and his mind going like Einstein's to boot?" I repeated, "Where in hell've you been?"

"There were a lot of details to clear up," he recoiled slowly. "I got back here as quickly as I could..."

"Details," I interrupted. "That's what I've been waiting to hear... What happened anyway. I know my part of it, but what else?"

He looked at me with a sudden compassion and removed his cap, rimming it slowly on his finger as he spoke. "Sure you want to hear it, Gil,...all of it? It isn't a very pretty story."

The thought of Toyoko came back sharply and I hesitated a moment before answering. "God, how I had loved her! Those irreplaceable times with her, those hours---days!" My hand wiped my forehead as I finally stuttered it out. "Is…is Toy….dead?"

"Yes, she is." It was as simple as that, but it tore at my insides as my mind tried not to register what he had said. "Your forty-five did a good job, Gil. It was quick. She never even knew."

No, she never knew. But I knew, as surely as I knew then that it would haunt me forever….

"I can't blame you for feeling the way you do about her. Neither of us ever had an inkling that she…"

"She was so real, Walt." My voice cracked as I got it out. "She was so real to hold and to love….I did love her Walt; still do. But why, that's the thing I just can't---."

"We had it figured all right, the only exception was Toy." He stood up and walked slowly around the cramped room as he talked. "It was she who forced her father into the racket, instead of him being forced to Hiamatsu and Duprey. You see, she met her real father, Duprey, in Tokyo while she was attending college. As to why she got into it, you can draw your own conclusion. There is no proof of that, but I prefer to believe that she was hooked into it and didn't do it willfully. At any rate, she was a terrific actor."

"Somehow I'm sure of one thing, Walt. I know when she was with me, well, that was no act then."

"Perhaps Toy did eventually change, in the sense that she may have wanted to get out of the business," Walt reflected calmly. "But even if that had been true, Duprey and Hiamatsu wouldn't let her. At least not alive. Remember when you made that crack about a girl like her having no business in a lousy school like that? You were right; it was just a front. I should have figured it out sooner, but I'm afraid I fell short there. Perhaps the same thing caught us both. She was beyond suspicion to us."

"What happened to you when you went in there, Walt?" I asked it listlessly, perhaps as an excuse to put Toy out of my mind. "Did you get the rest of the gang?"

"Well, I can praise the Lord for all that paint I had on," he smiled. "I got right into the parlor like a breeze. Hiashitani thought I was one of the pushers. I sat around with the rest of the outfit until Vette came screaming up with his sirens at full blast. Man, you should have seen the arsenal those boys dragged out then! Every damn one of them was loaded for bear! Anyway, I made my way to the door and drew my forty-five.

That was fine until I turned around and told them to drop their guns. I'm still not sure whether it was a left hook or a right cross, but I wound up seeing stars! It was a damn good thing Vette didn't wait to make his charge, or I'd have seen a hell of a lot more stars! Anyway, the pushers saw that they were out-numbered and most gave up. Hiamatsu didn't score so easy though; he shot it out. The last time I saw him, he looked like a screen door. You could see right through him except for the blood! We've got Hiashitani in a cell now, along with seven of the pushers."

"How about Duprey?" I asked with renewed interest.

"If things have worked out right, they should be locking him up in Singapore right now."

"What things?"

"Well, we notified the authorities in Singapore right after the raid, but they wanted to wait until they could catch him with the goods. According to schedule, he should be at the airport now with the stuff. That's where they're going to nab him. Anyway, I'll know for sure by tonight so I'll let you know." He stopped flitting around the room then and lit on the chair again.

"I suppose you heard my shot?" I looked at the wall as I asked it.

"I was in no condition to hear it myself," he answered, "but Vette was and he took off running. Lucky for you it happened after the other shooting stopped. Otherwise, you might not have been found in time."

"Yeah, lucky," I repeated to myself slowly. "For me, but not for her. I was trying to stop her and I could hardly see after she…" My voice fell off and I couldn't finish it.

"We found Chieako too," he added. "Knifed. Not a pretty sight at all. You must have seen her too when you came through the tunnel. There was more in the little escape hatch than her though – about a quarter of a million in heroin capsules."

"I didn't see it when I came through," I reflected quickly, "although I was in the dark quite a bit of the way."

"It was there all right, about half-way down the tunnel in a metal box."

We were both silent for a moment, then I said, "Anyway, I'm glad the whole thing was successful for you, Walt. Try as I will, I don't think I'll ever see it that way myself."

He looked at me with concern once more. "You might at least mull this over – if you hadn't stopped her, she could have made it out. If she had gotten away with the stuff, all our efforts would have been useless. With the evidence gone, we'd have had a hell of a lot of explaining to do to the Japanese police, and not even a leg to stand on. As it stands now, you can consider the saving of a lot of American servicemen. Take your choice."

I looked at him squarely then and replied, "I'm still an American, Walt."

He smiled and started to get up. As he did, his hand shot to an inside coat pocket and he fumbled around for a moment before drawing out several envelopes. He held them out of reach, tantalizingly, as he said, "Thought you might enjoy hearing from home. These have been lying around over at the section for several days now; hope any news inside isn't stale. He paused as he passed one of them under his nose. "With all that perfume, I'm certain that at least this one isn't…"

I reached out quickly and grabbed them from his hand, and he laughed as he stepped back.

"Thanks, Walt." I glanced at the return addresses on the envelopes, and when I looked up again, my 'eagle' had flown away.

CHAPTER TWENTY-THREE

Dusk was slowly settling in over the city as I left the train station and walked slowly up the street.

The people were everywhere, and as I walked, I wondered why I had even noticed their quaintness before. They were suddenly no longer the strange, yellow, slant-eyed people I had once read about in books. Now they were a people moving with a purpose in life as all persons do. Their customs no longer seemed strange, no more so than my own. They were a people who had been dropped into the depths and had risen with smiling faces – weathered, ripped and disfigured as are all faces who have known the adversities of life---faces from far away, and yet at home.

Suddenly I knew why Walt had been unable to explain this strange country to me, why he had said that it is a land of experience which one cannot hope to comprehend all in a day.

I glanced at the Takoma Hotel as I passed, and its lights still blinked on and off overhead. I stopped a moment and looked upward to the window where I had first known the love of Toyoko. Then, filled with torturous feeling, I tore my eyes away and walked onward.

The noise of the juke box and the crowd came from the Club First Chance and I tossed away an urge to enter it once more.

Finally I came to the side street and turned, leaving the giant Torii at the entrance of the shrine behind me.

Instinctively I took off my shoes at the top of the stairs before I entered the room. Everything was just as it had been that last night, but it was not a room filled with remorse. Instead, it was a room of love, where two people had lived and loved for what seemed like a life-time, and yet it had been so short a life-time.

The table and its chairs were intact and the picture still hung unjarred on the wall. I walked to the fusuma and opened the panel. The housecoat was lying there, together with several articles of my own and Toyoko's. Slowly I reached in, drew out the coat, and closed the door again. Very carefully, I rolled up the kimono and put it inside my shirt.

The bedroom panel was partway open and I walked through the doorway. The radio was on the stand beside the bed, and I controlled an urge to turn it on. As I did, an object beside it caught my eye. I walked over and picked up the ring carefully. Its large solitaire glistened in the wavering light. I clutched it in my hand as I moved toward the window. I pushed the curtains aside slowly and looked down at the yard. The new house was glistening with lights, and upon the steps two small children were playing with dolls. Their laughter could be plainly heard, and as I watched I could feel the tears slowly welling up in my eyes.

The sound of footsteps on the stairs brought me back to reality and I fought quickly to regain my self-composure. I turned around slowly to see Walt standing in the doorway.

"Mind if I come in?" It was a quiet, understanding question, and I had the feeling then that if it had been anyone else, I would have pushed them out the door.

"Sure, come on in, Walt." I faltered slowly as I turned back to the window. "It's a free country, I think."

He hesitated a moment before answering, and he didn't move from the doorway. "I think I understand how you're feeling, Gil, and I'm not one to intrude. But I'm leaving and I just thought---well, I thought you'd be here and I just wanted to say goodbye, that's all…If you'd rather, I'll go…"

"No!" I spun around and walked back into the living room. "I didn't mean it that way. I was just in a different world, that's all." I smiled as I sat down on the edge of the table. "I'm really thankful that you brought me out of it." I took out a cigarette and lit it nervously. "You're leaving, eh? Where?"

"New assignment. I'm not sure just where yet, but I have a feeling it will be Korea. He leaned against the door jamb and continued quickly. "But I have some news for you, lucky boy; you didn't get Korea, you're pegged for home."

"Home," I stuttered it out as I looked at him unbelievingly. "I knew I wouldn't stay here, but I thought maybe Korea."

"Korea!" he exploded with a laugh. "You mean you really wanted to go there? Hell man, you've fought your war! If you don't believe it, take a look at your battle scars in the mirror sometime! And don't look so sick; you're not being drummed out of the Corps, you're being promoted. In fact, you're even up for a medal of some sort! If that's all bad news, I sure wish it would have come to me!"

"I hardly know what to say, Walt."

"Then don't." He grinned as he stepped backward through the door and his hand shot up in a salute. "See you around, Pal."

The tiny gold bars glistened on his shoulders, and the fact that he was an officer suddenly struck me again. He was an officer, yes, but to me he still was and always would remain the pop-eyed, smiling little Corporal I knew as Walt.

"So long, Sir." I said, as I threw my right arm up in a salute.

"Walt," he grinned.

"So long, Walt." My arm dropped slowly and I watched the empty doorway a moment...I never saw him again.

I sat there on the edge of the table and finished the cigarette slowly. I wanted to think but thoughts would not come and when the smoke was gone, I rose slowly and walked out the doorway and down the stairs. I paused only a moment at mama-sans door, laid the ring gently on the sill, and rapped softly. I then walked through the doorway and into the street. I did not look back.

CHAPTER TWENTY-FOUR

They were warming the giant engines and the noise roared in my ears. Soon the plane would shoot down the runway and we would be in the air, headed for home...home. Unconsciously, I reached into my pocket and drew out the envelope. Once again, I unfolded it carefully and began to read:

Dear Gil,

I know that you do not think very highly of me now, and I cannot blame you for it. But I must tell you how I feel, and at least offer an honest explanation of my actions.

I know mother wrote you when she sent my ring, and I can imagine what she must have said. I want you to know that it was all true---it was then at least, but not now.

It was all so foolish of me. But Gil, I missed you so much. I did date another man. I'm afraid it even went farther than that and we thought of marriage. I couldn't go through with it, Gil, not when it came right down to it. Then I realized that I had used him to take your place, and I've felt terrible about it. I should have known that it was impossible long ago, and now that I do, I fear that it may be too late.

I love you, Gil, and only you. I can't say or do any more; it's all up to you now. I could hardly blame you if you were to burn this letter. I can only hope that you won't, and that somehow you can find it in your heart to forgive me.

I'll always love you with all my heart.

God Bless You,
Barbara

I put the letter back carefully and turned to look out the window. We were in the air and the land was falling away swiftly as we ascended.

The strange island I had known for so short a time was disappearing through the haze, as was the thought of Toyoko, who I had loved so dearly, yet perhaps not dearly enough. Ours had been a strange enchanting moment, one that would live on in my heart long after the tears and the anguish had passed on. Then the clouds closed over the plane and there was nothing left.

I turned and settled back in the seat and after several minutes, my eyes became heavy. As I dozed, the face of Barbara slowly focused. She sat smiling in the stands, the crowd was once again cheering the team on and the red and brown leaves were again falling in gentle spirals on the State campus.

THE END

By Ed Gilbert